D0719044

Coyote

How best is justice served – by the law or from the barrel of a gun?

A family is brutally murdered and their homestead burnt to the ground. The bodies are so badly disfigured that identity is difficult to determine, but one of the daughters is known to be missing. Is it eighteen-year-old Grace Mayfield or her younger sister, Chrissy?

The missing Mayfield girl must now be found and the killers brought to justice. Some say it was the work of renegade Cheyenne. Sheriff August 'Gus' Ward has his doubts, but evidence is scant.

When the mysterious shooting of a stock agent on the streets of Laramie is linked to those who may have been responsible, Gus is faced with the savage reality that justice might not be served unless he is willing to take matters into his own hands. If he does, is he still a man of the law or has he crossed the line to become an executioner, and no better than those he is willing to kill?

Coyote

Lee Clinton

A Black Horse Western

ROBERT HALE

© Lee Clinton 2018
First published in Great Britain 2018

ISBN 978-0-7198-2735-8

The Crowood Press
The Stable Block
Crowood Lane
Ramsbury
Marlborough
Wiltshire SN8 2HR

www.bhwesterns.com

Robert Hale is an imprint
of The Crowood Press

Typeset by
Derek Doyle & Associates, Shaw Heath
Printed and bound in Great Britain by
4edge Limited

For Lani

1

NIGHTMARE

The Awakening

She woke with a start, in panic, as if from a nightmare of being thrown into a bottomless pit. But fourteen-year-old girls don't have such disturbing dreams, do they? Not practical prairie girls like Christine Mayfield. Isn't their world one of pleasing, pretty things? Of coloured ribbons and lace, a new Sunday bonnet, the birth of the bay foal she'd named Candy? Pleasant, secure thoughts of her loving family – her parents, her grandmother, little brother Ben and her adored older sister Grace.

But no, this was no momentary hallucination from a bad dream. This was a vicious awakening and no matter how hard she tried, she couldn't catch her breath. A large hand pressed down upon her mouth with such force as to bend the bed boards beneath her head. A thumb and index finger clamped her nose tight and she could feel the abrasive skin upon her lips and cheeks. Panic took hold as the unshaven face above grinned.

She was being suffocated to death.

A yank on the hem of her nightdress pulled the cotton garment from between her legs. With jerks and tugs her modesty was being removed. Instinctively she gripped at the fabric to both sides of her thighs as she tried to yell for help and kick free, but she was trapped. With strength ebbing, draining and fading away, the strain in her muscles eased. *Dear Lord*, came the thought, may it be over soon. And with a sense almost of relief she felt the tension in her arms and legs wane as she relaxed and involuntarily wet herself.

'Chrissy,' came the scream from her sister. 'No, not Chrissy.'

It was the shout of her name, distant at first, then closer, that spun her back into consciousness. Grace was calling. She must answer. She twisted her head with a jolt and threw her hands up to the wrist of her assailant, grasping and pulling just enough to free his grip, open her mouth and suck in a breath.

A finger instantly stabbed between her lips, coarse and bitter, sliding across her tongue. Without hesitation, she bit upon it with all her might and ground her teeth to chisel deep into the bone as the warm taste of blood ran down to the back of her throat.

With a sharp yelp of pain the finger withdrew, to be immediately followed by a whack to the side of her head with such force as to hurl her out of the bed and on to the floor.

'Run, Chrissy, run.' It was Grace calling out, half muffled, with her face pushed down upon the bed. A man straddled her, his hand pressed against the back of her neck, as he grunted like a pig. 'Run,' came the scream from her older sister. 'Run, run, run.'

Chrissy leapt to her feet. Her attacker threw himself across the bed to grab at her nightdress, pulling it tight around her legs. Desperately she flung her fist back and struck repeatedly at his grip.

He let go and tried to clutch her wrist.

It was a moment of untethered freedom. She knew that she must not hesitate. It was the briefest of chances, her one and only opportunity to escape – and she took it.

'Aaron,' came the shout, 'quick, she's getting away.'

Chrissy sprinted on bare feet out of the room and down the hall towards her parents' room, yet all speed seemed to disappear. It was as if she was running across a flooding creek in waist-deep water, an illusion of a spinning mind trying desperately to escape and survive. Chrissy was a good runner and she was now in full flight and sucking in deep breaths.

From her parents' bedroom door came the flash and blast of a pistol shot. She smelt the burnt powder and saw the silhouette of her father tumbling to the floor. In fright, Chrissy Mayfield ran on, through the open front door, across the porch and into the night that came upon her as black as coal. But she knew every obstacle before her.

At the front gate another shot echoed from within the homestead. Dashing left towards the barn the sound of thumping boots upon the path was close behind her. She was being chased.

Racing on, turning left again, down the side of the house and past the water pump, she leapt over the horse trough and dashed towards the cattle yard. Fast pounding footsteps were gaining on her now. Then whack, thump and grunt as her chaser collided with the trough to sprawl headlong upon the ground.

She made it to the stockyard and scrambled on all fours under the fence as a shot cracked just above her head to wallop into the railing, splintering wood and bark. Back on to her feet and hitching up the hem of her nightdress she sprinted, hunched, into the night, while a coyote called as if to say, over here, this way.

Two more shots followed in quick succession, each just inches above her head.

On and on she raced, with burning lungs, to the sounds of three more shots. Two very near, just to the right, each a crack to the ear. The last shot struck the ground near her heel, missing by only an inch. The lead bullet distorted and whizzed up to flick the back of Chrissie's running leg. It stung like a whiplash, but while it would bruise and ache, fortunately it did not lacerate the skin.

Somehow, Chrissy Mayfield had been spared. Yet each of those six shots was fired with the deliberate intention to kill. It was as if an invisible hand had guided her to safety.

'Did you get her?' came the shout. 'Did you get her, Calvin?'

'Little bitch bit me,' was the response.

'But did you get her, Cal? Did ya?'

Chrissy ran on, her feet beating a rhythm to a chant, 'Calvin, Calvin, Calvin, the other man, Aaron, Aaron, Aaron.' On and on she ran into the safety of the night, to where the prairie lands crease into gullies and ravines that can hide and conceal, and where the coyotes run free.

2

STAINS

Two Days Later

When Grace Mayfield missed her meeting with her betrothed, Deputy Sheriff Henry Ward, and Reverend Jacob Brown of the Laramie Episcopal Church, Henry was no overly concerned. While Grace was punctual by nature and Monday was the Mayfield pickup day for supplies, life as a settler brought with it numerous uncertainties. Priorities could shift on the strength of the wind. Unforeseen tasks, big or small, often required immediate attention, especially where livestock were concerned. If she missed the appointment then there was a good reason, and that would be explained as soon as she was able.

With just the family to help, her father Abe had to depend on the women in his life. His wife, his mother, who lived with them permanently, and the children. And of those three offspring, it was Grace and Chrissy who were the fittest. Baby Ben, a late and unexpected arrival, was aged just three years, while Chrissy was maturing into a strong young woman now just shy of her fifteenth birthday. She would soon take over the chores and duties of her older sister Grace, who at eighteen was promised. Wedding plans were already well under way, even though it was still ten weeks away from the chosen date. Grace would then move to Laramie to live with Henry's family until their new cottage could be built. Family-to-family agreements had long been discussed and settled. Grace would continue to pick up the weekly supplies from the general store and take them out to her family in the Wards' buckboard, stay overnight and return the following day. Taking away such an able body as Grace from her family and the demands of the property was certainly going to have an impact. However, they would manage, of course. They always did.

All the Mayfield women, regardless of their age, were industrious. They could ride, rope, fix a fence and change the leather washers in a hand pump. And none more so than Chrissy. She might be young but she was capable. And like her mother and her gran, she could bake. It was their talent and proficiency, be it a pie, a tart, a cake, cornbread or sweet biscuits. All baked to perfection.

On Tuesday, by mid-morning, Henry had become preoccupied and fidgety. Grace had yet to arrive in town. Young men are known to be impatient at the best of times, especially those about to enter matrimony. His father, Gus, who was also his immediate superior as the sheriff of Laramie, on a little urging from his wife, Martha, suggested that Henry might like to ride out to the west. 'Just to check on the settlers,' Gus had said, which of course included the Mayfield family. And if along the trail he was to meet Grace on her way into town, well, he could turn around and escort her.

Henry immediately agreed, and with haste went down to the livery stable, selected a three-year-old Morgan of fifteen hands, saddled up and departed. He cut across the back of the cattle yards to save time and from there he picked up the road west towards the Black Hills.

The conditions supported a fast ride. The day was cool, the sky clear and the wind light. The surface below his mount was firm, well-worn from settler traffic over the past few years, and it was likely that he would come across a friendly traveller or two.

But caution was still required.

It was just the year before last that Cheyenne had stolen cattle over near Fort Fetterman and burnt out several ranches. The Army had taken the swift reprisals demanded by the settlers, which in turn had led to a truce and a treaty. Ownership of the Black Hills was given to the Lakota, forcing a peace by pushing the Cheyenne further north.

Well, almost a peace.

Some renegade Cheyenne were less than happy to abide by the agreement. They owed no allegiance to Red Cloud, the Lakota chief, even when entering his land uninvited. Still, no matter how fragile, peace was peace and most settlers welcomed the possibility.

In just over two hours Henry came to the small hill that overlooked the Mayfield homestead. He would be with his beloved in just a matter of minutes. His heart skipped a beat and he drew in a quick breath, telling himself to settle, act naturally and remember to speak slowly. And remember to call his soon to be mother-in-law Frances, not Fanny. This was on the advice of his mother, who understood not only the importance of etiquette, but also the need for respect when preparing to join a new family.

Henry glanced down and began to brush the dust from his sleeves to make himself look presentable. With his horse now riding easy, he cleared the crest to where he could see the Mayfield property and the miles of prairie beyond. He looked up, hesitated, and stopped his brushing and fussing. His brow creased with confusion; the homestead had gone. He knew exactly where it should be, but it wasn't there. Nor was the barn.

'What the—?' was Henry's bewildered response.

He pushed high in the saddle and glanced around. Was he on the right road? He felt disorientated. The homestead had vanished as if into thin air. He leant forward and all he could make out, where it had once stood some mile and a half ahead, were the water pump and the trough by the trees, and two dark stains upon the ground.

'Oh, no, please. Please God, no. No, no.'

His heels thrust back hard and his mount took off down the slope, kicking dirt and dust high from galloping hoofs. And all the time Henry continued to call to himself, 'No, not this, not this, please God. Not this.'

3

THE LAW

Later That Same Day

When Henry's father, August 'Gus' Ward, saw his son, it was at the end of a hard twenty-mile ride back from the Mayfield property in just over ninety minutes. His horse had done forty miles in all that day, and was spent to the point where it looked ready to drop. Henry was in no better shape; he was close to being incoherent. Tear streaks cut tracks in the dust on his cheeks, and he was so distressed and inconsolable that his mother had burst into tears when he was finally able to convey to her what he had seen. It was something Gus had never observed before. His wife was stoical by nature and also practical in character, but he knew why she was so upset. The future of her son's planned life with Grace had also turned to ashes.

When Gus was finally able to settle his son, the news was devastatingly clear. With the fire, the homestead had been totally razed and there was no sign of life. 'Gone,' Henry repeated over and over, 'All of them, gone,' while shaking his head in disbelief.

Gus went straight to the livery, returning Henry's horse and saddling up a fresh mount for the ride out to the Mayfield property. It was in the middle of this familiar act, as he was pulling up on the cinch, that he decided to take Henry with him. To leave him with Martha in both their current states would do neither any good. Henry had missed the horrors of the war by the skin of his teeth, turning eighteen on the day after President Lincoln's killing. He had also been spared the violence that comes with a brutal death. Since his swearing-in as a deputy almost two years ago, his experience had mostly been of the mundane, with just a few fist fights in between. Yet it was inevitable that the reaper would come close sometime soon. Especially if he remained in the service of the law, although that profession had never been a foregone conclusion.

Gus and Martha were proud of their son and only child, but both knew that on the surface, Henry seemed like a poor fit for the law. He was polite and quiet in manner, and at first glance, his appearance could easily be mistaken for that of a young clergyman. Yet he had always been diligent and self-reliant. He could track, shoot and skin with effortless efficiency, and he could be determined; he had shown that when pursuing his duties as a deputy. But what his father valued most was his son's honesty and loyalty. In many ways, he was his mother's son. She was a woman who was resolute yet forgiving, and that was what was needed more than anything in these times when the wounds of war remained deep and raw. Gus knew that time healed, but five years on from the cessation of fighting was nowhere near long enough. It would take generations, and Henry and Grace were part of that next new generation.

Grace Mayfield would make the perfect wife for his son.

Gus and Martha had discussed it at length. She may have been five years younger than Henry, but she was mature beyond her years and as tough as a man in mind and spirit. She was a daughter from a true family of the West. That their son had found her, particularly in this territory dominated by men, was more than a minor miracle.

Gus rode back from the livery to the office with two fresh horses and left instructions, businesslike as always, before departing. He told Ivan Davies, his senior deputy, that the Mayfield property had been razed and that Henry had found no sign of life. He confirmed that Joel, the second deputy, was due back later that day from doing his rounds down south. Both Ivan Davies and Joel Ferber were experienced and capable lawmen whom Gus felt at ease to leave in charge. It was Henry, the third deputy, and the youngest, who had the least experience. However, any time that Henry spent away from the job would impact on the other two deputies. Gus advised Ivan that he was taking his son back out to the Mayfield property to assist him, before saying, 'This has knocked Henry hard, he's going to need a little time.'

Ivan understood and nodded before asking, 'You want me to notify the mayor?'

'Yes, of course,' replied Gus. 'Best to get the word out via the mayor before the rumours start.'

'Indians?' questioned Ivan.

Gus shrugged. 'Would seem so, but I don't know. It was either an accident or deliberate and that's the first thing I need to determine.' Gus turned to go, then stopped. 'Better let Barrows know as well. We'll be needing their services.'

J. B. Barrows & Son was the town undertaker.

Ivan nodded again as Gus left. He then took the key from the wall to lock up the office before leaving to find the mayor down at the rail yards where his principal employment was that of station agent. And on his walk towards the station, Ivan mulled over what Henry must have found. He thought it best that Gus kept his boy under his wing. This was not going to be an easy day for Henry.

Truth was, it would not be an easy day for Gus either.

4

MADNESS

The Investigation Begins

Gus pulled Henry up short, before the gate to where the homestead had once stood. The small, now ridiculous fence still defined the outer perimeter of where there had once been life. To one side were the horse trough and the water pump, next to a tall grove of tamaracks that had been seared by the heat of the fire. The barn was also completely gone, like the homestead. It had once stood some fifty yards away and the bare ground between the two ruins clearly signalled that this was no accident. The two buildings had been deliberately torched separately, but for what purpose? If to destroy evidence then what evidence? What was the cause of this tragedy? Was it theft of goods or livestock? Was it vengeance against the settlers? Or was it something else?

'Just wait,' said the father to his son, signalling Henry to remain mounted. 'I need you to point out to me where you went, so that I can distinguish your tracks from the others. We need to investigate carefully and just take one step at a time.'

Henry drew in a deep breath and started to speak, only to immediately stumble over his words. He stopped, looked down and his eyes filled with silent tears.

Gus sat quietly and waited, before saying, 'Try again, Henry,' as he reached across and placed a hand upon his son's shoulder. 'I know this is tough, but we have a job to do. Just take your time.'

Henry took a second breath and began to explain how he rode up to the fence, entered through the gate, and—

His eyes showed a flash of confusion. He wasn't sure. Did he walk around the ruins? Yes, but was it to the right or was it to the left? He couldn't remember.

'Did you step into the ashes, Henry? Just think. Did you step into the ashes?'

No, he hadn't. For some reason, it had seemed wrong to do so. He had just looked. He was stunned, he told his father. 'I just couldn't believe it.' He eyes started to fill with tears again.

'OK, we'll start from here and you walk with me, but just behind. I want you to record notes. Take out your field book and lead pencil.' Gus didn't think Henry would manage the task, but it didn't matter, it would keep him occupied.

Gus dismounted and motioned to Henry to do the same. Then slowly, he edged forward towards the gate, searching the ground, picking up the first signs of foot traffic before squatting. He glanced at Henry's boots then looked ahead. He could clearly see his son's fresh tracks and waited and watched as his eyes slowly started to decipher the numerous other marks, scuffs and prints that littered the ground. He stood, took two paces to the left and squatted again. He turned and looked back at their two horses ten paces back, then across to the right to pick up Henry's original horse tracks before turning back to examine the ground near the gate, just to the left.

'Three horses,' he said. 'Tethered to the fence, just here.'

Henry was in a daze and did not respond.

'Henry, let's get on the job. Note, three horses.' Gus rose and stepped forward, slowly examining the ground as he went. When he had passed through the gate and down the path to where the porch and front door had once been, he stopped and squatted again.

He had been in this house on several occasions and cast his mind back to what once had been. To the right was the front room and he remembered how it had looked with its careful charm and comfort. There had been the furniture, which had once belonged to Agnes Mayfield, Abe's mother, and bequeathed to Fanny. Abe had tanned some mule-deer skins and mounted the antlers that graced the wall above the fireplace.

To the left was the front bedroom. He had never been in that room, but had caught a glimpse from the hall of the large wooden bed. It was now gone. In its place, he could see two mounds in the ashes. He knew what they were; the remains of Abe and Fanny Mayfield. But they were not side by side where the bed had stood. They were towards the door. Had they been trying to escape?

Directly behind that room was the nursery where Abe's mother, Agnes, and baby Ben slept. Gus now walked to the left, waving to Henry to follow, then turned to his right at what would have been the side of the homestead. He stopped where the small window to the nursery had once been. He could see the broken glass on the edge of the ashes. Gus knelt, lowered his head to examine a burnt mound immediately to his front. It was the remains of Agnes, and the small bundle against her was Ben. He had died in her arms.

The lawman lowered his head and spat upon the ground. 'Christ,' he said under his breath, before standing to continue his slow passage around the ashes, frequently stopping to crouch and search inch by inch with his eyes. His last stop was the remnants of the room directly behind the front room. This was the girls' room which Grace shared with younger sister Christine, or Chrissy to all who knew her. He began the ritual again, bending low and running his eyes over the ashes, and there, just to his left, was the black tell-tale pile. It was one of the girls, but which one? Could anyone ever tell? He doubted it. The fire here had been intense as the room backed onto the storeroom where the lamp oil and cooking grease were kept. He continued looking. But no matter how hard his observations or positions he chose from which to view the site, he could not find the remains of a second body in the girls' room. Why?

He retraced his steps back to Henry who was standing near the water pump. He seemed frozen to the spot, as if in a daze, with his field notebook in hand and pencil poised, ready to write in an instant.

Gus took him by the arm and walked him back to the horses. 'Just stay here,' he said to Henry. 'I need to look around.'

He then returned to the ruins and circled counter-clockwise, searching for the sixth body. Could one of the girls have perished in another room? He looked and he looked, but there was no sign. He then walked slowly over to the barn to examine the ruins and while the odd item, mostly metal, like the hubs and springs from the remains of the buckboard, and the anvil near the small forge, were clear to see, there was no sign of deceased life, not even livestock. By the barn door, now marked by the bracket hinges upon the ground on the edge of the ashes, he

22

could see the remains of a kerosene lamp at an easy arm's throw from the entrance.

Gus turned and retraced his steps back towards the homestead fence. Some twenty paces back and looking towards the stockyard, he began slowly to inch forward, searching the ground as he went. It was just before the very corner of the fence that he saw it. An imprint, not the whole foot, just the ball of a bare foot where toes had dug into the dirt to gain purchase for the runner. He walked on slowly and picked up the second print, more pronounced this time where the runner had leapt over the water trough. Then a third imprint clearly marked upon the soft damp ground on the other side of the trough.

Gus looked up in the direction it was heading, towards the cattle yard. 'Henry.'

No reply.

'Henry, come here, quick, son. One of the girls is missing.'

Henry arrived in an amble, notebook and pencil still held in front of him.

'Henry, listen to me.' He shook his son's shoulder. 'One of the girls managed to escape.'

Finally, Henry seemed to come alive. 'Grace!' he said.

'Not sure. But you need to collect your thoughts. We need to get a search party out here, but it will be dark before I can get back to Laramie and get one raised. I want you to start the search now, on your own, from here. Can you do that?'

Henry was nodding.

'Let me hear it, Henry. Can you do that?'

'Yes,' said Henry, his focus and confidence slowly returning. 'Yes, I can.'

'Good boy, good boy. Now, start nice and easy, looking for any sign. Take it slow. Walk your horse and mark where you go. Camp up when you can no longer see, and listen up. Call out both Grace and Chrissy's names as you go, and be back here no later than two hours after sunup tomorrow. By then I'll be back with the search party.' Gus paused. 'Got that, Henry?'

'Call Grace's name as I go.'

Gus went to correct him, but paused and thought it best just to leave it at Grace's name. 'Right, Grace.' He didn't want to complicate matters any further. His son was already having trouble coping. Gus then added, 'If Cheyenne did this, they'll be long gone. Still, best to keep your rifle loaded and close at all times, just in case. I'll stay for a little to help get you started before I head back. Remember, we've got a job to do, so stay keen and alert.'

Henry nodded.

Gus wanted more from Henry, but it was the best he could hope for at this moment, under these circumstances. Besides, he also had much to do and much to think about, as a voice inside kept asking, what the hell has happened here? What has caused this madness?

5

REMAINS

Talk of Cheyenne

When Gus returned with a search party of twelve the following morning, Henry was waiting, alone. He confirmed, with a shake of the head to his father, that nothing had been found of the missing Mayfield girl, either dead or alive. Each man dismounted and walked over to Henry to offer their condolences with a comforting handshake. Then under the gaze of the men who had volunteered their time to search, Henry listed the steps he had taken. From time to time he referred to his field notebook on distance and direction and advised on how he had marked his trail.

When he finished, one of the men said with authority, 'Cheyenne.'

'Maybe,' cut in Gus, 'but let's not get ahead of ourselves. We will conduct a methodical search for a young woman on foot in a state of distress, who may be hiding or unable to find her way back.' Before anyone could butt in, Gus continued. 'We'll conduct a fan search to the left and right of Henry's initial line of search. Don't rush, as you may miss tracks or signs. Five men to each of Henry's flanks as he moves forward to show where he searched yesterday and early this morning. The two remaining men are to act as outriders. One north, the other south for one mile each, then west for five miles. They will mark the limit of the search for today and look out for any sign where riders may have entered or left the range. Depending on what's found, the search will then be extended as necessary. Henry will be in charge.'

'What about you, sheriff?' came the call.

'I'll assist the undertaker. He's due here within the hour.'

It was a sober reminder of what had to be done and seemed to subdue those who may have wished to waste time. They all looked at the ruins with the realization that there were bodies within those ashes. None would want the job that Gus and the undertaker were about to do, so they got about dividing the tasks that had been issued, each man willing to be employed as was best.

Gus led Hyrum Barrows, the son of J. B. Barrows, who had titled his family business as Laramie Undertakers of Distinction, over to where the front door of the homestead had once stood. He pointed out each of the charred mounds to the undertaker and advised him as to who he believed them to be.

Hyrum accepted Gus's deductions without question and the two started with the remains of Abe and Fanny. What was left of each rigid body was disfigured beyond recognition. The two men gently lifted each corpse on to a well-worn wooden stretcher, marked with the faded stencilled words 'Property U.S. Army Field Hospital'. When taking up the stretcher with the second body, it tilted to one side and the burnt remains slid off and back into the ashes.

Gus apologized. 'My fault,' he said, 'I got distracted.'

Hyrum silently lowered his end of the stretcher and began to roll the cadaver back on to it, briefly stopping to look more closely at what was left of a blackened hand pressed across the body. 'This one is Fanny Mayfield. I can see her wedding ring.'

As Gus bent in to look, the smell of burnt flesh caught in his throat. He could just make out the dark gold band upon the stump of a blackened finger with a white protruding bone.

'My Lucy said that Fanny was most proud of that,' said Hyrum. 'It had belonged to Abe's grandmother, and been given to her by Agnes.'

Gus looked again at the small engraved band with its fine pattern.

'Valuable,' the undertaker added.

Valuable, thought Gus and lifted his head to get some fresh air from a slight breeze that brushed past the side of his face. 'Valuable to no one now,' he said, not knowing what else to say.

'It will be valuable to the missing Mayfield girl, if she is found.' It was said as a matter of fact.

Gus repented. 'Of course,' he said, feeling unsettled, and wondered why this was so difficult. He'd been exposed to the sight of slain bodies on the battlefield and later as a sheriff, but this was different. Was it just because these were people he knew personally – a family that was soon to join with his? Or was it because they were innocent? They were not soldiers who'd died in battle, or hot-headed cowboys who thought they were fast with a gun. These were just settlers – God-fearing, hard-working, settlers. 'Of course,' he said again, 'the missing Mayfield girl.'

The bodies of Agnes and Ben could be identified not just by their location within the ruins, but also by their physical size and weight. They were glued together at first, until Hyrum prised them apart, exposing a patch of unburnt clothing. It was Agnes's nightdress and light blue in colour.

When it came to where the girls' room had stood not even Hyrum could confirm if it was Grace or Chrissy who had escaped the inferno. The limbs below the knees and the elbows were missing, due the intensity of the fire, and the head was little more than a skull.

When they respectfully placed the remains of the unknown Mayfield girl on to the undertaker's buckboard, Gus asked, 'Do you ever get used to this?'

'This?' questioned the undertaker as he pulled the tarpaulin over the remains. 'If I did, there'd be no need for me to look into the bottom of a whiskey glass.' And once again it was said as a matter of fact.

Gus drew in another deep breath of fresh air. 'This was harder than I thought it was going to be.'

'How's your boy holding up?' asked Hyrum.

'Better today,' replied Gus. 'Well, at least for the moment. He's hoping that it is Grace out there.'

The undertaker nodded as he tucked the tarp into the sides of the buckboard. 'Do you think it was Cheyenne?' he queried.

Gus hunched his shoulders, 'Looks that way, but I need to talk to the agent and see what he has to say.'

'Some in town are already saying it's Cheyenne.'

'Who in particular?' asked Gus, expecting to hear of some vague tittle-tat from gossips unnamed.

'Rufus Cole and the Moy brothers were telling all who would listen to them in The Blood last night. Said it was renegades from up north and that they must have been

28

after white women.'

He was a little surprised to hear names. 'Did they say how they knew this?'

'Nope. It was just saloon talk as far as I could tell.'

'In their saloon?'

The undertaker jumped down from the back of the buckboard. 'That's right, in The Blood.'

Gus knew the undertaker was a drinker, but after today he would no longer pass judgement on this habit to imbibe. How else could he be expected to cope in this line of work? 'I'll talk to the Indian agent first and see what he has to say,' said Gus.

'Good idea. I can't see how those brothers would know any more than you or me. I've never trusted them. Do you?'

'I trust the evidence, I have to. That's my job as a lawman.'

'Good luck with that,' said Hyrum. He gave a grunt and climbed up on to the seat of the buckboard. 'I see the stock is still yarded.'

Gus glanced across to see cattle standing around the gate of the stockyard and more heading up the slope behind them.

'They're looking for water,' observed Hyrum.

'I'll check the troughs,' responded Gus.

'If it was Cheyenne the fences over there would be down and the stock gone.' With that the undertaker flicked the reins, nodded a farewell to Gus and departed with his pitiful cargo of burnt human remains.

Gus gave the undertaker a wave as he stood pondering. No, he did not trust Rufus Cole or his two younger half-brothers either. Their saloon, The Red Blood, was aptly named. On a Saturday night, it could sometimes turn into a fighting pit and had earned the reputation that more blood had been spilt there than at the Bulls Head Market in Chicago. Colourful words, but with an element of truth. At least once a month, Gus and his deputies had to attend to a pay-night brawl that spilt over into the street. He'd spoken to Rufus regarding his responsibilities not to break the peace, but his point of view was one of casual care at best. He said he was providing a service to the railroad men and cattlemen who worked hard and needed a place to let off a little steam. In reality, Rufus added to the steam. If the crowd got too rowdy and looked like trouble, he'd cut off the liquor and throw them out onto the street.

But that's not where the trust had been lost between Gus and Rufus.

Cole and his half-brothers had lied to him about the character of a young woman who had died on their premises from a fall out of an upstairs window. The body had been carried back inside and laid on the floor of the vestibule by the time Gus arrived to investigate. They said she was a dove touting for trade without their knowledge, who had accidently fallen while calling out to would-be customers in the street below. Yet the evidence proved that she had no prior convictions of any kind, and had arrived on the Union Pacific the previous day from Omaha City with an ongoing ticket to Salt Lake City for the following morning. The doctor confirmed that her neck had been severely broken from the fall and apart from bruises to the left upper arm, no other marks or lacerations were on the body. The whole affair left Gus with suspicion and resulted in a sort of Mexican standoff where he waited for their next move, which was yet to come. Maybe they weren't directly involved, considered Gus a little later, but he also knew that sometimes he was often too quick to give the benefit of the doubt. Such charity was an unfortunate part of his nature and not always compatible with being a lawman.

6

SHOT

Pondering

Gus left the ruins of the homestead and rode west to catch up with the search party. He prayed that they would find the missing Mayfield girl soon, while the weather was good, and before thirst or injury could take its toll. And he prayed even harder that it would be Grace who would be found.

He knew this was a selfish thought. What if it was young Chrissy out there lost, frightened and desperate to be found? But he was also desperate in his heart for his son, who had taken this hard. In fact, it had unsettled him. Gus knew where this could lead. He'd seen similar during the war, at Halltown, after a fighting withdrawal that resulted in nearly three hundred casualties on a single night within the 2nd Division. For some of the young reinforcements in his company this was their first taste of action, and they had become so rattled by the indiscriminate hand of death that they had withdrawn into themselves for sanctuary. As a senior sergeant, Gus had found himself having to console and persuade these desolate youths of the need to hold both their line and their spirit, which most finally did, but not all. Some became so lost within themselves that they couldn't even remember that they now belonged to the 6th Vermont Infantry. They just wanted to go home, wherever home in Vermont was, and some couldn't even remember that. It was an unravelling of the mind. For Henry, finding the destruction of the homestead and the Mayfield family had resulted in a similar impact. Fortunately, he had pulled himself together when addressing the men of the search party that morning and Gus knew why. It was hope. While there was hope, Henry could focus and keep despair at bay. But for how long? Optimism under these circumstances was at best fragile.

Gus also thought of Martha, who had taken to Grace on that first meeting, just over a year ago, as if she was one of her own children. His wife had told him, with almost a sense of relief, 'That Grace Mayfield is going to be Henry's saviour and a match made in heaven.' Now her world, too, had been dealt a savage blow – she had lost the daughter she had always yearned for.

These thoughts now spun and rattled around Gus's head as he rode, while also wondering, even if Grace was found alive, would things ever be the same again?

Of course not, was the answer, he knew that – nothing ever was, but you just had to get on with life. Gus shook his head, a gesture instinctively made, as if to clear such wandering thoughts. He just needed to take one step at a time – and that first step was to find the missing girl before she died of exposure to the elements or from injury. Because then, and only then, would he know for sure what exactly had happened and who the perpetrators were. And that had to be *his* sole focus if justice was to be done.

He met up with the search party just after noon. They

had stopped and regrouped to take a little water. Ben Edmonds from the Laramie General Store was handing out some dried apple strips and Bent crackers, 'A new line,' he said, that had come in from Massachusetts. Noah Fillmore, who worked as a clerk for the district court, suggested they should be called soft tack, as a reference to the hardtack they all knew from the war. Gus took a bite, savoured the salt and listen to the banter. It saved him from having to ask the question, 'Found anything yet, boys?' because the answer was clearly, no.

Gus stayed on and helped in the search for the rest of the afternoon but was careful to hang back. He needed to show to one and all that Henry was in charge, and it needed to remain that way. He would soon have to return to Laramie so that he could speak to Doc Larkin regarding the formal identification and the issuing of death certificates. Once done, the Mayfield remains could then be released to the undertaker for burial. Gus would also have to speak to the mayor about funeral arrangements, as no member of the family was now available either to arrange or pay for the formalities. He also needed to bring the mayor up to date with the devastation he had found at the homestead. And then there was the Indian agent; he needed to speak to him.

An hour before last light, Gus rode up alongside Henry to let him know that he was heading back. His son had that fixed determined look that men get when worried and concentrating hard, or what some say, are thinking too much. Three of the search party were also leaving to return to town but would be back later the following day with camp supplies. Gus's departing farewell before he left for Laramie was to assure Henry that he would chase up additional men to join in the search. What he really wanted to say was 'I love you, son', but those words were not spoken between men, so he gripped his boy's upper arm briefly and shook his head slightly. It was a parting gesture, a silent signal of affection.

Gus arrived back in town around eight. By the time he was eventually to get home to his cottage on Clark Street, it was close to midnight. This was due to several important tasks that required immediate attention before he could see and console his wife.

The first of these was the mustering of more men for the search party. He rode over to the east side of the Laramie River and walked around tent-town calling in on those he believed were available to spend a couple of days or more away from their employment. After two hours, he had arranged for seven extra men to join the search over the next three days. Of course, they all hoped that they might not be needed and that the missing Mayfield girl would be found tomorrow or the next day at the latest.

Gus then went to find the mayor to provide his report. They discussed various matters, which included a description of the Mayfield property as it now was, and how the first day's search had gone. One of the last matters discussed included the need to raise funds from the community for the cost of the burials.

'It can't be anything fancy,' said the mayor.

'It didn't need to be,' said Gus, 'But,' he added, 'it does need to be done with dignity.'

The mayor gave a soft 'humph', which Gus took to be light disapproval, so he decided to nip it in the bud straight away, just to put paid to any unnecessary penny-pinching. 'The bodies are so badly burnt that we don't know which Mayfield girl is missing,' he said softly. 'We were only able to identify young Ben because of his size and that he was cradled in his grandmother's arms.'

The mayor got the message; Gus saw it in his eyes. He was horrified at the thought. As a man who had remained in the service of the railroads during the war, he'd had no experience of violent death.

'The livestock on the property will also need attending to,' said Gus. 'I've watered them but they need to be checked on.'

'Livestock still there?' questioned the mayor. 'None taken?'

'As best as I can tell. The top yard is just about full.'

'I'll speak to the livestock agent first thing tomorrow. Abe did all his buying and selling through Larry. He'll know what needs to be done.'

Next stop was to see Doc Larkin, who had already examined the bodies. There had been no change to the identification of the corpses of Abe, Fanny, Agnes or Ben that Gus and Hyrum had already been able to determine. It was the fifth body that would have to be buried in an unmarked grave for the moment, until it could be determined which Mayfield girl had survived.

'And if we don't find her?' asked Gus.

'It will have to remain unmarked as I'm unable to issue a conclusive death certificate.'

Gus could feel the invisible weight of responsibility on his shoulders as he said, 'Then we need to find whoever is missing, so her sister can rest in peace.'

The doctor showed his agreement with a single nod before saying, 'I have one other thing I need to discuss with you, but it can wait till tomorrow. It's late and you've yet to have supper. You also need a good night's sleep.'

'What is it?' asked Gus.

'It can wait,' reiterated Doc Larkin.

'Important?'

'It can wait.'

'I need to see the Indian agent first up then get back to the search. I'll be pressed for time.'

The doctor was reluctant but finally relented. 'All right. But you better sit a while.'

Gus pulled up a chair. 'Go ahead.'

'Every one of the remains has suffered a gunshot wound.'

Gus felt his stomach roll and lift as if to rise into his throat before saying, 'Good God, everyone? Including young Ben?'

'Including young Ben. I'll make out a full report for the court. Best you go home and rest.'

When Gus stepped onto his cottage porch, Martha heard him and came to the door. He went to talk, but couldn't get the words out.

Martha asked, 'Have they found her, Gus?'

He shook his head and put his arms around his wife and held her tight, pressing her to him, his head over her shoulder so that she couldn't see his tears of despair. But Martha could feel the tremor of sorrow in his body and clutched him tight, her hand gently rubbing his back as if to comfort an infant.

7

THE INDIAN AGENT

Fate

Gus couldn't sleep. He'd eaten next to nothing, yet he felt as if indigestion was coming on, high up in his chest. When he got into bed he couldn't settle. It was as if every inch of his body was on edge. Muscles seemed to twitch, tighten and cramp, forcing him out of bed on one occasion to rub the back of his calves. And between the blankets again, no matter how he lay, he just couldn't get comfortable. He knew that Martha wasn't sleeping either, even if she was lying still and locked in her own thoughts. When tiredness did eventually overwhelm body and limb, it was close to dawn and he descended into a deep, yet unsettling sleep. By the time he woke he felt spent. He was also late for the schedule he had planned.

Martha was long up and out the back in the wash house heating water for the weekly laundry. She offered a cooked breakfast, but coffee was all that he could face. They sat in

37

silence at the small table, each connected by thoughts of how easily the serenity they had finally managed to achieve, after all these years of struggle, had been snuffed out like a lone candle flame.

Gus left to visit Albert Leonard the Indian agent just before ten. Al had been sent out by the Department of the Interior to assist in the consent of the Lakota Treaty, and as one of the few to speak Sioux fluently, Chief Red Cloud of the Lakota had asked him to remain after the signing of the truce. The Department in Washington had agreed to the request and it was a smart move. Al had served as a Union officer during the war and had credibility with the Army, which generally had little time for the civilian Indian agents. Many in the military only knew one way to prevent conflict between settlers and Indians, and that was to kill Indians. There was also some residual ill-feeling inside the uniformed ranks, from back when the Bureau of Indian Affairs was taken from the control of the Department of War and given to the Department of the Interior. Al now helped to bridge that gap.

He was a well-travelled and educated man who had worked as a surveyor in Panama before the war. He was quiet by nature, thoughtful, and one of those straight talkers that just dealt with the facts at hand. He didn't speculate and his conclusions were always reasoned. In fact, in many ways he was much like Gus in attitude, yet the two didn't know each other well as there was mostly no need to mix or meet, especially since the Lakota Treaty had come into force. One thing Gus did appreciate, however, was the difficulty of Albert Leonard's line of work.

The accommodation of Indians, regardless of tribe, was half-hearted at best by the majority of settlers. The reality was that both sides eyed each other off with suspicion. The

Mayfield killings and the search for the missing girl would quickly add to further mistrust and resentment. The mayor had said as much, and how could it be otherwise in such a tight-knit community, where the rumour of a Cheyenne raid to capture girls for slaves was a consistent topic? This common view was based on past raids against settlers across the Territory, so another raid was more than plausible. Yet Gus had the unexplained feeling that something just didn't add up. He didn't know why but he felt it in his gut. Was it intuition? Or was it just a dyspeptic stomach?

Al had heard of the Mayfield deaths and the burning of the homestead from the mayor, not that long after Gus had departed with Henry to commence his investigation. In response, he had sent off two Lakota scouts, who worked directly for the office of the Indian Agency, with a message to Red Cloud seeking assistance regarding any information on Cheyenne movements. In particular, any renegades from up north who were out to steal livestock.

'And have you had a response?' asked Gus.

'Yes, the scouts got back just before first light this morning with the word that there are no Cheyenne warring in the Territory.'

Gus was sceptical. 'Is that reliable?' he asked.

'Yes.' It was an unequivocal answer.

The look on Gus's face showed his doubt.

The Indian agent responded. 'I trust Red Cloud and I trust Little Wolf. If any Cheyenne did come down here to raid, they would be renegades acting on their own.'

'Then how would Red Cloud know that Cheyenne renegades were raiding across Lakota country?'

'Chief Little Wolf still has eyes and ears within the renegades and he would tell Chief Red Cloud.'

'Why?' asked Gus.

'Lakota and Cheyenne have much to fear from the consequences of an attack on settlers. The current treaties would be jeopardized and Army reprisals would follow. Little Wolf and Red Cloud both want peace; it provides them with a place to live and hunt. And that's pretty much all they want, at least for the moment. Most townsfolk and settlers can live with that arrangement. Not all, but most. It's a balance with at least a modicum of goodwill from both sides, but that could evaporate if the white folk thought that Indians, any Indians, were back on the warpath.'

'But just say,' said Gus, 'if Cheyenne renegades did come down here to raid, what would they be after?'

'Livestock. Horses, cattle, but only in numbers they could handle and drive quickly, and driving cattle all the way up north would slow them down, so in reality it would just be horses.'

That made sense to Gus. 'And women, would they be after women as well?'

Albert Leonard paused before he confirmed, 'Renegades will take white women.'

'Will they kill and burn as well?' asked Gus.

'You know they will. Why are you asking?' replied Al.

'It looks like the work of renegades, but all the fences are in place and the livestock are untouched as best as I can make out. They started wandering up to the top yard looking for water while I was there. Of course I'll have to check, but to my eye it seemed to be about the same number of head that I saw when I was last out there talking to Abe and that was only two, three weeks ago.'

'If you get a headcount to the livestock agent he should be able to confirm one way or the other. Abe Mayfield would have purchased and sold via the agency. All the settlers out west do.'

'The mayor is going to speak to
livestock,' said Gus as he rubbed
'Could this just be Cheyenne reneg
trouble between Lakota and the sett

'If that was so then the Lakota wo

Gus still wasn't convinced that Re
'Rumour has it that it was Cheyenne
sort of talk will disturb the settlers a

The Indian agent shifted uncomfortably in his chair
then put both elbows on his desk. 'I know. So the question
is,' said Al, 'if it's not Cheyenne then who is it?'

'I have no idea,' said Gus. 'Abe didn't have an enemy in
this world. At least to the best of my knowledge he didn't.'

'For both our sakes, we need to find out and soon,' said
the agent.

As Gus got up to leave, he stopped, reluctant to speak,
but it had to be asked. 'If renegades do have the Mayfield
girl, how much time do we have before they—' He could-
n't bring himself to say the word.

Al knew of Grace and Henry's planned wedding, everyone in town did. His mouth tightened before he finally
said quietly, 'Too late. It would have happened as soon as
they were clear of the property and knew they weren't
being chased.'

'Her fate after that?' asked Gus. 'Would they kill her?'
He did his best to disguise any possible hint of relief in his
question.

'No,' said Al, 'they would make her a slave to fetch
water, cut and carry wood.'

'And would they continue to use her?' asked Gus.

The Indian agent didn't say a word, he just looked at
Gus, his elbows still upon the desk with his hands clasped
as if in prayer.

8

SEARCHING

Hope

Gus was back out at the Mayfield property by early afternoon and about an hour later he caught up with the search party eight miles to the west. Their tracks were clear to follow where the horses had beaten a path back and forth to where the homestead had once stood. They had also set visual markers that pointed to both the direction and extent of the search. These were small strips of rag, like limp ribbons, tied with a simple thumb knot to bushes every eighth of a mile to mark the trail. If found by the missing Mayfield girl, it would lead her towards the search party or those travelling back and forth within the search area.

The first group Gus caught up with was led by Noah Fillmore, the district court clerk. With him was Ben Edmonds from the general store. A bunch of cotton strips protruded from his top pocket. The conversation was brief and gloomy. They had found no recent sign of anyone or anything at all.

Gus quizzed, 'Not even Indian?'

'No,' they both said together. Then Ben added, 'Maybe we are just searching in the wrong spot. If it was Cheyenne, they would have gone north and we've been searching mostly west.'

'Surely some sign would still have been found,' offered Gus. 'They would have to go west first to catch her because that's where the footprints were leading. Then they would head north.'

Both Noah and Ben agreed that the search had been wide enough to pick up any such sign, like a party of Indians, especially if they were also driving livestock.

'Let's just hope that the Indians didn't go after her and that she's still out here, lost or gone to ground, injured,' said Noah, with Ben nodding in agreement.

It was clear to Gus that they both firmly believed that it was Indians who had killed the family and burnt down the homestead. And why not, he thought. What other explanation could there be, regardless of any denials from the chiefs?

Gus didn't get to see his son until Henry rode into the makeshift camp that had been established another two miles further to the west and some ten miles from the ruins of the homestead. It was an agreeable site beside a small creek with a good flow of clean water coming from a rocky ravine immediately to the north, which had been christened with the name Coyote Canyon, as a family of prairie wolves had come into the camp on the first night of occupancy and stolen some food. Henry was the last man to arrive and it was just on last light. He dismounted, and workmanlike, immediately began doing the rounds and speaking to each man – fifteen in all – seeking reports on the areas searched and marking them on a makeshift map in his field notebook.

When Gus finally got to speak to Henry it was also businesslike as he handed over two saddle-bags that had been filled with provisions of beef jerky, dried fruit, potatoes and slices of cold pudding from his mother. Henry put one of the bags over an arm and proceeded to walk around offering each man a choice. This gave time for Gus to observe his son, and he was somewhat surprised. He could see the tiredness and concern etched upon his face and in the firelight he looked as if he had instantly aged by some five years. He was also looking thinner than he had ever remembered. This prompted Gus to discuss provisioning for the search party.

Henry advised that this had been taken care of. Nat Crenshaw had returned to Laramie earlier that day to ask his father-in-law to bring out his chuck wagon and to take on cooking duties. They expected him back later the following day.

What Gus was trying to say to Henry was that he needed to eat and keep his strength up, but the message was lost, so he asked about where the provisions were coming from.

'Ben sent Nat back with a note to draw the provisions he needed from the general store,' said Henry.

'Good,' said Gus, 'I've spoken to the mayor about funding for—' He was about to say, for the funerals, but quickly changed course and said, 'for the search.' Gus then added, 'Have you thought of a lay day?'

'Sunday,' said Henry.

Gus knew he couldn't skirt around it any longer. 'The funerals are planned for Saturday. It can't wait any longer.'

Henry said nothing.

'You'll be going back?' Gus asked.

'I wasn't planning, unless I have Grace with me,' said Henry. 'I'll keep searching till then.'

'Sunday too?'

Henry nodded.

'On your own?'

'If needs be.'

'I see,' said Gus and he knew that now was not the time to enter into a discussion of the rights or wrongs of going to the funerals, or staying out here to search on his own. Instead he said, 'Do you want me with you?'

'No,' said Henry, 'but if you could attend the funerals for me and pay my respects while I keep looking for Grace, that would be appreciated. I don't want to leave her out here on her own.'

'Of course,' said Gus, as he had no idea what else to say.

Gus and Martha attended the five funerals on Saturday, as did most of the town. It was a sombre affair as each body was lowered into the ground, side by side, after the calling of the name and the reading of a prayer. Tears openly flowed when Ben's small coffin was interred, and again for the last casket as the words were said, 'A Mayfield daughter, known only unto God.' On completion of the service, collection plates were passed amongst the congregation and over two hundred dollars was raised, some fifty dollars of that coming from Rufus Cole and his two half-brothers Calvin and Aaron Moy. Many commented on their community spirit and generosity.

Over the following days more men and supplies arrived at the camp, which had now been given the name Harmony Creek. The search was extended to the north and even a little way to the south. No need was seen to search to the east as that's where Laramie lay and had Grace, or even young Chrissy gone that way, they would have walked back into town by now.

Martha began a regular trip every second day out to the

Harmony Creek camp to deliver supplies from the general store, hand over freshly washed clothing items sent by wives, and collect dirty laundry. She also took back any messages and diligently wrote up a notice that was pinned on the church bulletin board. It advised one and all of how the search was progressing in terms of the area covered, which now stretched out some forty miles west and thirty-five miles north. She also listed the name of every man who participated and the number of days each had attended.

Gus commented to Martha how smart it was for her to recognize those who were giving up their time, often at the expense of a wage, to join the search.

Martha replied, 'I didn't do it for that.'

'What did you do it for?' he asked.

'To shame those who have yet to lift a finger.'

There was a hardness in his wife's eyes as she spoke. One he had not seen before.

At the top of each report posted, Martha wrote the date and the number of days searched. It was now at Day 14.

9

PRECIOUS TIME

The Coming Chill

The days were now becoming just a little chillier on the high plains, especially in the mornings when the central fire at Camp Harmony had yet to be stoked. Fall was well on its way and not that long after, the first fresh snows would appear upon the Medicine Bow Mountains. Yet, regardless of the chill, or the number of days into the search, Henry was up before anyone else in the camp to put on the coffee and entice the searchers to rise for at least one more day.

However, the truth of the matter was, as each day passed, the numbers began to dwindle, and who could blame them. They had searched far and wide and now day twenty-one had passed with still no sign of the missing Mayfield girl. Martha kept up her routine to support her son, and in a way, it relieved Gus of having to spend too much time away, as law-and-order matters in Laramie still required attention. Some of those duties were fixed by date and place, especially on court day, when charges were heard and evidence had to be given.

Rumours of Cheyenne renegade involvement in the Mayfield killings had now hardened. It didn't seem to matter that no evidence of any Indian involvement had yet to surface, either from the Indian agent or from the return of the 2nd Cavalry to Fort Laramie after patrolling far to the north. All the while Gus's indigestion continued to annoy him, like a repetitious shout from the gut, saying something wasn't right.

But what, exactly?

If it was Cheyenne renegades, why had no sign been found by the searchers? Fast-ridden horses leave clear tracks. Al Leonard personally met with Red Cloud to discuss the matter, and once again he was given assurance that if a white girl or woman had been taken, then Little Wolf would have known and passed this information on. So, if it wasn't an Indian raid, it had to be an attack from an as yet unsuspected source.

Gus approached Judge Chester E. Morgan of the Laramie District Court and sought his advice after passing on the little information he had gained from his investigations so far. Judge Morgan listened intently before saying, 'Terrible business this, Gus. Best it is tidied up as soon as possible. I also had Larry up here yesterday seeking authority to sell the Mayfield stock.'

Gus went to say, tidied up how, but instead he just confirmed that the matter of the stock also needed to be resolved, before asking what would happen to the proceeds from the sale.

'It will go towards Abe's estate, but held by the Territory until probate can be enacted.' The judge then asked Gus, 'Do you know of any kin?'

'No,' said Gus before correcting himself. 'The missing Mayfield girl, the money can go to her.'

The look on the judge's face indicated that he thought

such an eventuality was now a very dim possibility. 'I'll speak to the bank and see if Abe secured his Will with them. If so, it may mention kin.' The judge made a note in his leather-bound diary, the scratching of the nib upon the page making the only sound within the room. The cold silence was finally broken when the justice said, 'If you don't think it's Cheyenne, then the other thing I can do is write to the Supreme Court and request any information that may have come before the courts regarding a similar event. It could just help you identify the culprits. Things like this are normally never isolated events, they have a history.'

Gus left the judge with the thought that tidying things up as soon as possible, to bring the perpetrators to justice, was now starting to fade considerably. Would it eventually elude him? Townsfolk had concluded, almost to the last woman and child, that it was renegade Cheyenne. The comment he most often heard was that the Army should raid the Cheyenne camps to the north to see if they were holding any white women. When Gus reminded them that renegades were being turned away by peaceful Cheyenne, and that women and children lived in those camps, it did not change their minds one jot. Seems rough justice was better than no justice at all, even when delivered against the innocent.

Gus dwelt and pondered on every aspect of this 'terrible business' as the judge had called it, but found that he was getting nowhere. He hoped that some fact or detail would emerge and set him straight. Maybe the judge's letter to the Supreme Court would provide that answer. However, in the meantime, he had to worry about the here and now.

He met with Larry Earnshaw of the Laramie Livestock Agency, who confirmed that no stock had been taken from the Mayfield property after an audit had been conducted pending sale of the cattle and horses. In conversation, Gus learnt that the stock was in good shape and had been moved down to graze by the main creek that ran through the entire length of Abe's property. In fact, his land had sole access to water all year round; therefore his neighbours had to lean on Abe's goodwill to gain access to water for their livestock. Permission to traverse had been given willingly, said Larry, who then went on to praise the Mayfield women, who could all ride like men, he had said, including Chrissy. 'Those girls are good with cattle and horses. They did most of the mustering for Abe by driving the cattle to the top yards on those days when a neighbour needed to get their stock to water. I've seen Chrissy do that on her own. She's a good handler by any standard.' He then went on to confirm that the Mayfield stock would soon go to market.

'Will it fetch a good price?' Gus asked in passing.

'Depends,' says Larry. 'Most buyers know that all the stock has to be sold regardless, so they will hold their bids, expecting to get a better price. But there is plenty of interest.'

Gus expected it would be from the meat packers in the East. 'Chicago?' he asked, referring to the Union Stock Yards.

'No, local,' said Larry.

'Who?' he asked out of curiosity.

'Rufus Cole for one.'

Gus was more than a little surprised. 'What would Cole want with a herd of cattle?'

'To build up his own stock.'

Gus didn't know that Cole owned any stock. 'I didn't know his business extended to cattle.'

'It's a new venture,' said Larry a little awkwardly. 'As a businessman, he keeps an eye out for any opportunity that may come along.'

10

ONE MORE DAY

Running out of Hope

As the days passed, the hope of finding the missing
Mayfield girl faded. Some were now openly saying that if
she was found, maybe it would be better that she be found
dead instead of having to live with what might have been
done to her. Gus didn't hear any of this directly. Instead it
was passed on by his deputies, who thought that he should
know, and they were right. He just didn't want Henry to
hear such talk.

A reply was received by Judge Morgan to the letter he
had written to the Supreme Court in Washington. It was
hand delivered by a US Marshal on his way to San
Francisco on the Union Pacific. The efficiency of such a
quick and personal conveyance impressed Gus no end
when he was called by the judge to the district court
rooms. The judge opened the correspondence, but
handed it to Gus to read first. It was just a one-page reply
that said, in a fancy sort of way, no, they had no such information of similar circumstances that could relate to those

described, but to rest assured that should any such word come into their possession, they would pass it on with haste. Gus handed the letter to the judge.

'Not much help, is it?' was his comment on reading the correspondence.

'Not much.' Gus couldn't hide his disappointment.

'Feel like you're running out of hope?' said the judge.

'Pretty much,' confirmed Gus.

'Know how you feel,' said the judge. 'Each day reduces the odds and is a day closer to the end of the search.'

Gus didn't sleep well that night. The realization that the time had come when it was now inevitable that the search would have to end rested heavy upon him like a weight on his chest. The community had responded and tried their best, but he could no longer expect them to keep it up. If the search was to continue that responsibility now belonged to the family. Many families in the past had searched on for years – some were even successful – but most were not. The sober truth in this instance was that there was no Mayfield family left to accept such an obligation. The closest to any known kin was Henry, who was betrothed to Grace.

Just two days later the mayor declared that all official searching would end after one month. The money had all but run out to pay for any more provisions and day thirty of the search was due to fall on the coming Sunday, when it was planned to dedicate a combined community church service to the Mayfield family and the searchers.

On Wednesday Martha made her last delivery to the camp. The quantity of provisions on the buckboard was small as there were few left in the search party. On Thursday the chuck wagon departed, leaving Henry with just six men before they, too, would ride back on late Friday or early Saturday morning.

However, when those last searchers did arrive back in Laramie late on Friday evening, it was with news that Henry had stayed behind. He had told them that he was planning to head west to where General Rawlins had camped in '67, then north to Fort Casper as he continued on with the search.

Gus knew he couldn't let his son do this. To search that far and wide was not only futile, but delaying the inevitable. It was worse than looking for a needle in a haystack. At least a found needle would make itself known by a sting and a jab to draw blood from a hand sifting through straw. A scattered search by one man could pass over a vital clue without notice. Henry now needed to stop, to finish his grieving, and return to his duties as a deputy.

Gus departed with his sombre thoughts before first light on Saturday morning and just managed to catch Henry by minutes. His son had cleaned up the camp, packed up the remaining provisions that were left after filling his saddle-bags, and was readying to depart.

A father now had the difficult task of disallowing his son's plans. 'I can't let you do this, Henry. It is time to come home,' he said.

Henry kept preparing his horse and avoiding eye contact.

It annoyed Gus. 'Did you hear me, Henry?'

Henry continued to adjust and tie down straps.

'I said, did you hear me, Henry?'

'I heard,' came the chilly response.

'We need to head back home.'

'You head back,' said Henry, 'I'm staying. I'm going to continue this search till I find Grace.'

Gus could feel his ire rising. He wasn't getting through and it showed when he said abruptly. 'What if it's not

53

Grace? What if it was Chrissy who escaped – and what if she's now dead? It's been a month of hard searching, Henry, and nothing. The chances of finding her alive are—'

Henry was now staring hard at his father, his hands still on the buckle of the saddle-bag.

Gus felt ashamed for his outburst, but he knew that he had to put an end to the search. It was like a battlefield amputation where the limb had to be sacrificed to save a life. It was going to be brutal – he had no choice. 'Judge Morgan has written to the courts in Washington for advice on any similar attacks against settlers that could be linked; and both the Indian agent and the cavalry commander have sought information from Chief Red Cloud and Chief Little Wolf on any missing white women. All have drawn a blank. I wish it were different, if only to end the unknowing, but nothing, Henry, nothing. It is time to let go or this will lead you to despair.'

Gus could see the tears welling in Henry's eyes. His words had stabbed and hurt deeply. His immediate response was to step forward and grip his son in a hug. He felt his boy's body shaking with grief as a coyote howled from up in the ravine and another howled back.

'Can I have one more day?' asked Henry. 'Just one more day.'

Gus was concerned it was a ploy. If he left Henry here and returned to Laramie, could he trust him not to head north? 'There is a church service tomorrow,' said Gus, 'to pray for the souls of the Mayfield family. We should attend, Henry. The town will expect to see both of us there, our families were close, and many will wish to offer their condolences to you personally.' Gus hesitated, then reinforced, 'You need to be there, the service is also for those who searched.'

Henry appealed. 'I'm only asking for one more day.'

Gus was about to strike out again and say, *For what purpose, for what possible reason?* but he held his tongue. Instead, he said, 'One more day, Henry, that's all. Just one more day. We will search together till last light, spend the night here, then depart early tomorrow morning, before dawn, to attend the service.'

Henry slowly nodded his agreement.

Have I compromised too much, thought Gus, or did one more fruitless day in the grand scheme of things really matter? Henry wanted no stone left unturned. Could he deny such a request? At least it would be time with his son and right now, that was more precious to Sheriff August Ward than anything else in this world.

11

ONE LAST SEARCH

A Signal Shot

Gus asked Henry to go through his field notebook and explain to him the extent of the search. Each page contained comprehensive notes, written small, in a clear hand. Towards the back, on a double page, Henry had produced a map of fine detail that showed the areas covered, along with dates.

Henry's proposal was that they ride to the furthest western point of the search and start from there. Gus knew that they had less than ten hours of daylight left, so he raised the concern that a lot of time would be used up travelling to and from that point, without contributing to the search.

Henry was insistent. 'We could search right up to dark and stay out there overnight.'

Gus's concern was that if they did overnight further west, it would lengthen the journey back to Laramie the following morning, making it almost impossible to be back in time for the church service. 'Let's just look for something a little closer, first,' he said, not wanting to upset his son. But it was difficult to see where, since most of the map was marked as searched.

When two coyotes called to each other from the ravine, Gus looked up instinctively, then back at Henry's notebook. He pointed to a spot on the page just above where Camp Harmony was marked. 'Has this ravine been searched?'

Henry glanced at his notebook then looked up along the creek to where the waters disappeared past some large smooth rocks as big as a barn. 'No,' he said. 'We couldn't get the horses up there.'

'Still needs to be searched,' said Gus, trying not to sound too enthusiastic, but it was perfect; the search could start immediately, be done in the time available, and add not a yard in distance for the journey back to Laramie.

'It will have to be done on foot,' cautioned Henry, 'and I think there might be more than one ravine.'

'Fine,' said Gus. 'We don't have to search the same ravine together, we can take one each as we go. We can travel light, we don't need to carry water, we have the creek. Just need to take a rifle should we need to signal each other, in case of a fall. It could be quite rugged once we get up there a little.' Then he remembered to add, 'Or if one of us finds something.'

Henry was mulling over the proposal.

Gus needed to break the silence. He wished he hadn't said, *find something*. Find what? Human remains fed upon by animals? 'It has to be searched, Henry,' he said.

'Yes,' said Henry, almost reluctantly as he looked at his notebook, 'it has to be searched.'

The climb along the river was a little tougher than first expected. The only semblance of a trail to follow was a narrow animal track. Footing had to be carefully chosen as a misstep could easily end in a tumble down between the large rocks that crowded the ravine, which at times obscured the creek. But the sound of the running water could still be heard, and it was this source that gave life to this enclosed world. It fed the creeping mahonia, the silver wormwoods and the cliff-bush, as well as the roots of the fir trees.

As predicted, and about two hundred yards up, the ravine split into two separate ravines that seemed to run parallel to each other. Henry took the ravine to the left, while Gus the one to the right.

Both of these gorges were similar in size and separated by a narrow ridge, which in time would be completely eroded by melting winter snows to become just one larger wide ravine, similar to the one they had just climbed through. Gus slowly squeezed his way between and over the rocks while searching for any sign. Animal tracks were plentiful, mostly coyote, who had made this their home, and he could appreciate why. It was difficult terrain for any of their predators, man or beast.

Henry too, had to step carefully, as his path was not just over broken ground and large boulders, but a number of fallen fir trees that lay directly across the bottom of the ravine. Green needles were still visible on the upper branches of the largest tree as it clung to life, its roots exposed to the elements with just a precious few still in the soil.

By mid-morning both Henry and Gus were about four hundred yards further up each ravine. Henry had spied some small caves off to his left. He was considering if they warranted inspection when his eye caught sight of a small white strip. It seemed to be not unlike the cloth ribbons used to mark the search trail. He immediately wondered if someone from the camp might have already conducted a search. After all, Harmony Camp was always occupied with at least one other man besides the cook, to help out where necessary, and not all the chores would occupy a full day.

When Henry picked up the strip of fabric he was unsure if it had been one of theirs after all. Certainly, it looked out of place, so how did it get here, he thought? Was it taken by a bird, plucked from a brush by a meadowlark, then discarded in flight? Or had it been placed here on purpose? He turned the cloth over in his hand and inspected it closely. It was free of any print or dye, a common bleached calico, plain-woven and used for so many purposes around the home, yet it felt soft. He rubbed it between his finger and thumb, as if caressing and urging the fabric to communicate.

A coyote called just a little further up and snapped him out of his ponderings as he placed the strip in his top pocket and pushed on.

Around midday Gus stopped at a small waterfall to drink and catch a breath. He stood his Winchester upright against a flat rock, took off his hat and fanned his face with the brim. From his shirt, he took some dried beef and began to chew.

The shot from Henry's rifle echoed up from his ravine, taking Gus by surprise. It was either a signal for help or something important had been found.

Gus picked up his rifle and pulled down on the lever, loaded a round and fired into the air to advise Henry that he'd heard his signal and was on his way. He didn't re-cock his rifle, but left the spent cartridge in the chamber. Gus seldom carried a rifle with a live round in the breech. There was no need unless he was hunting, be it an animal or a felon. He'd seen too many men maimed from the accidental discharge of a loaded firearm.

He looked up the near sheer slope of the ravine for the

easiest way to get out. It was at least sixty feet in height and would require dexterity to traverse, but it was the quickest way to get to Henry and this was the route he now chose. With deliberate steps, he began his climb, rifle in hand as he moved from rock to rock.

About halfway up and having difficulty with his footing, Gus heard the second shot. He was in no position to signal back, so he pressed on, wondering what Henry had got himself into? Or maybe Henry hadn't heard Gus's shot and was trying to get a response? Or had Henry found—

His foot slipped.

Gus nearly lost his grip on his rifle as one leg swung out into space some thirty feet above some disturbingly sharp broken rocks. He gripped tight at his handhold and took in a deep breath. 'Easy, just one step at a time,' he said quietly to himself. 'Just one step at a time.'

For the next agonisingly slow ten minutes, Gus carefully inched his way up to where he could now reach over the top edge of the ravine and laid his rifle down. This finally gave him two free hands to heave himself up. He was just about there when the shale under his fingers started to give way. Gus was now in great danger of tumbling backwards into the open ravine and onto the rocks below. With all the effort he could muster, he began to pump his legs and paddle his arms. He was now a scrambling man trying to run up a vertical wall sideways, but somehow it worked. He was just able to claw his way to safety. When Gus rolled on to his back to catch his breath, it was not lost on him what might have easily happened and he thanked the Almighty for his deliverance, just when the third shot was fired.

Quickly he got to his feet, still out of breath, and started to jog back along the narrow ridge towards the sound of the signal. After about one hundred and fifty paces, he caught sight of Henry, some fifty feet below in the next ravine with his rifle to his shoulder ready to shoot.

Gus followed the line of sight of Henry's rifle, tracking it to the other side of the creek, and there, some fifty yards away, was the figure of a girl in a torn calico nightshirt standing on a large flat rock, surrounded by a pack of coyotes.

12

BODY AND SOUL

Home

The words, 'Good God,' spilt from Gus's lips. There, in the clear light of day, was a figure, below him but not more than eighty yards from where he was standing, and it had to be Chrissy Mayfield. She looked unkempt and dirty in a tattered nightdress, but it was more than her appearance that gave this view from Gus's elevated position a dream-like quality. She was perfectly still, frozen, with a pale arm held up as if to stop Henry from firing a shot, and all around her, very close, were coyotes.

Gus glanced at Henry below him with his rifle held to his shoulder. Instinctively Gus raised his Winchester so that he too could protect Chrissy from the prairie wolves. But the dogs also seemed frozen in place. Gus counted seven of them, all alert, standing or sitting and facing Henry, and none were paying any attention to Chrissy.

Another shot cracked through the still air, to echo up the ravine towards the mountains. Gus could see that Henry was trying to scare off the wolves, but his shot just caused the dogs to edge a little closer as if to protect her. It was an incredible sight, and all the while Chrissy held up her palm to Henry.

'Don't shoot,' yelled Gus. 'They are too close to Chrissy.'

Henry glanced up.

Gus lowered his rifle and waved back.

'I've called her to come to me,' shouted Henry,' but she won't.'

'Then you'll have to go to Chrissy. Just do it slow and careful and I'll cover you from here.'

Gus went down on one knee, rifle to the shoulder as he watched Henry advance towards Chrissy. His son stepped cautiously as he edged his way towards the creek, and all the while Chrissy and the coyotes watched intently. The only sound to break the silence was the odd stone that slipped to clatter from beneath Henry's foot.

When he had crossed the stream and was within twenty paces of Chrissy, Henry placed his rifle gently upon the ground, and with both arms out, tried to entice her to come to him, but she wouldn't move. Slowly, he stepped forward, speaking quietly, 'It's me, Chrissy, Henry. Remember? Henry. You know me.'

When he was just ten paces away, the dogs began to move, each slowly circling around Chrissy to almost brush against her legs, before calmly walking on up a narrow trail that wove its way alongside the creek. As the last dog passed, with the sunlight shining upon the flawless brown and grey coat, Chrissy lowered her hand and touched its head, all the while looking at Henry. As if to say goodbye, the mountain coyote nuzzled her hand for a second then departed.

Henry launched himself forward and embraced Chrissy in his arms, hugging her tight.

Gus watched and should have felt relief but he knew immediately something was wrong. Chrissy made no response whatsoever. She just stood, arms by her sides, head turned and looking to where the coyotes had disappeared.

The walk back down the ravine to Camp Harmony now alarmed Gus as Chrissy did not answer one of their questions. In fact, she hadn't uttered a single word. Henry held her hand to guide her, but each time he let it go, it fell limp by her side, and he had to reach down to take the hand back. But it was the look in Chrissy's eyes that worried Gus the most. It was as if she was asleep, but with her eyes open. It was unsettling.

By the time they arrived back at the campsite, it was too late to depart for Laramie. Gus got the fire going and prepared a hot meal, while Henry sat close to Chrissy.

When handed a plate of beans she seemed disinterested and while she looked slim in her nightshirt, she didn't look undernourished. And all the while, not a word passed Chrissy Mayfield's lips. She neither asked for food or water, nor offered a response when so provided.

A bed was made close to the fire, between Henry and Gus, as the evening was showing a chill. Around midnight, Gus woke to the howl of coyotes up the ravine, only to see Chrissy sitting up and listening, and for just a moment, he was worried that she was going to get up and head off towards their calls. So, he got up, placed his jacket over her shoulders, stoked up the fire and remained on watch.

They departed just before first light, leaving behind the last of the provisions in order to travel as light as possible. Henry said he would take Chrissy on his mount for the first part of the journey home and she seemed to draw comfort from the horses, touching both gently on the nose before Gus gave her a hoist. He could feel the hardness of the skin on the sole of her foot as she mounted behind Henry to sit on his bedroll. Gus had to take each of her arms and pull them around Henry's waist to get her to hold on. Finally, she gripped her hands together and lay her head against his son's back. Gus remained concerned, but he did concede that at least she looked comfortable and warm in his bulky jacket.

When they passed the Mayfield property, Chrissy showed no response. Her face was turned in the direction of the ruins, but her unblinking stare seemed not to recognize where she was. Gus offered to take Chrissy, but Henry now saw no reason to make the change as they were travelling slowly, for both the comfort of Chrissy and the horses.

When they arrived in Laramie it had the eerie presence of a ghost town. The community had turned out in full for the church service for the Mayfield family and to thank those who had assisted in the search. Gus didn't want to take Chrissy near the church in her current state, concerned that she might take fright at the sight of the crowd and any unwanted attention, but there was little choice. He had to get Chrissy to the doctor and Doc Larkin would be at the service, as would Martha, the other most important person he could think of to attend to the waif now in his and his son's care. Gus told Henry that they should ride across to the church where he would quietly slip inside, unnoticed, and get the doctor and Martha. In hindsight, it was a foolish plan, which became clear not long after they had crossed into Ivinson Street. The crowd was so large that it couldn't be accommodated inside the church and now spilt out of the front doors and into a large pool of people. All were there, regardless of faith, joined as one to remember fellow settlers who had been wickedly slain, a missing daughter, and those who had searched for her.

It was the young Curtis boy who was standing on a buckboard so that he could see, who rang the bell on Gus, Henry and Chrissy. He saw the horses approaching, squinted for a moment, recognized the sheriff and the deputy, then just as Henry turned his mount towards the church, Lenny Curtis got a clear view of Christine Mayfield. From the buckboard vantage point he yelled at the top of his voice, 'Look, they found her and it's Chrissy. They've got the missing one and it's Chrissy, not Grace.'

The initial reaction from those closest to the buckboard was to give young Lenny a harsh look as he was known to pull a prank or two. But when their eyes shifted to the approaching riders where they could clearly see Chrissy, a giant roar erupted from the crowd. This, in turn, caused those packed into the church to spill out to see exactly what all the commotion was about.

Gus immediately realized that a calamity was now unfolding as people started to swarm in their direction. He quickly told Henry to head for home and that he would bring the doctor and his mother straight away. 'I won't be long,' he called. Henry turned his horse, while one hand clutched Chrissy's wrist, and made for home.

Gus was about to dismount when he realized that he would be swamped, so he walked his horse through the crowd and dismounted directly on to the buckboard. 'Doc Larkin,' he shouted, 'has anyone seen Doc Larkin?'

'Where did you find her, sheriff?' came a shout.

Gus kept searching the sea of surging faces, desperately looking for Doc Larkin.

'Is she hurt?' came another call from the crowd.

'Doc Larkin, has anyone seen Doc Larkin?' he called again.

Finally, Gus saw a waving hat. It was the doctor doing his best to get to Gus.

'My wife? Has anybody seen my wife?

'Over here, sheriff.'

It was Noah Fillmore pointing just off to his left. Gus caught sight of Martha's green bonnet. He pointed and mouthed the word *home*, and she responded by waving her hand and immediately made off in that direction.

When Doc Larkin arrived at the tray of the buckboard, Gus knelt and said above the noise of the crowd, 'Henry has taken Chrissy Mayfield back to our house. Could you attend to her?'

'Of course, of course,' shouted the doctor above the noisy crowd as he tapped Gus on the side of the arm to confirm that he understood.

As soon as the doctor was clear of the gathering, Gus called for quiet and obediently the crowd silenced. 'Can you hear me?' he shouted. Hands waved in reply from the back. 'Henry found Chrissy Mayfield yesterday afternoon,' he continued to shout, 'not far from Harmony Camp. Seems she may have been hiding in a cave further up the ravine.'

'Is she OK, Sheriff?' came a yell.

'She still seems to be in fright, but—'

'Poor girl,' interjected one of the women in the crowd.

'The doc is going to check on her and she will stay with my family,' continued Gus.

'Damn Indians,' came another yell. 'That's why she is in fright.'

These sentiments stirred the crowd as another called, 'Cheyenne, that's who,' and heads nodded vigorously. 'Sooner they are all killed off the better.'

It was getting ugly.

'Settle down,' yelled Gus. 'We'll find out exactly what

happened from Chrissy, but first we need to give her time to rest. And we need to thank the Lord for her deliverance.'

Enough heads nodded for Gus to see that the message was getting through to some, and that should have given him a little confidence. But he felt uneasy. Was it his dyspepsia returning or was it a deeper concern? Had they brought back the soul of Chrissy Mayfield or just her empty body?

13

PECULIAR

Agreement

Gus had been home for a good hour before the door to the bedroom opened and the doctor and Martha appeared. Concern was etched on their faces.

Gus waited, not asking, but preferring to be offered an explanation.

Doc Larkin moved away from the closed door a little and in a low tone, said, 'She's not been touched, so we should be merciful for that. However—'

Martha cut in quickly to excuse herself, so that she could draw a bath for Chrissy.

'Yes, of course,' said the doc.

'However?' asked Gus.

'However, she seems to be in some kind of malaise. To be expected in a way. A month out there, on her own, yet surprisingly her physical condition isn't too bad. Youth helps of course. She has lost some weight but not as much as I would have expected.'

'Did she talk?' asked Gus.

'No,' said the doctor. 'Not a word. Did she say anything to you?'

Gus shook his head, 'No, not a word.'

'We just need to give her time. It is a wonderful healer, time.'

Gus felt a little annoyed that that was the best medical advice on offer. 'Do you have any other thoughts?' he asked.

'I think she is still suffering the effects of losing her family. I think she may have observed some shocking happenings.'

'That I don't doubt,' said Gus, 'but will she be able to identify who attacked and killed her family? If it was Cheyenne?'

'If it were Cheyenne,' said the doc grimly, 'they would have had their way with her. And she would have had to escape, and I don't think that happened. Especially if it were renegades. Regarding her physical condition, however—' Doc Larkin paused as Martha came back into the room. 'That is a surprise. She must have scavenged food from somewhere. But where?'

Gus had asked himself the same question, as it was hard to believe that anyone could have survived for that length of time without showing severe signs of malnourishment. After much thought on the ride back to Laramie, he could only come to one conclusion, which he now decided to pass on to the doctor. 'I think she was getting provisions from our camp. We found her just close by, within daily walking distance.'

Doubt showed on the doctor's face. 'If that was the case, then why didn't she make herself known to her searchers?'

'Because she didn't go into the camp.'

The doctor now looked confused. 'Then who did?'

Right at that moment Gus felt reluctant to say, but he

had no choice, no matter how foolish it sounded. He had to tell them both what he had observed. 'I think a family of coyotes may have taken food from the camp for her.'

'What?' said Doc Larkin in amazement.

'The camp was at the bottom of a ravine. Further up was home to quite a few coyotes. You could hear them, close by, calling of a night. And on occasion, they got into the camp and stole from the provisions. The boys christened the ravines Coyote Canyon.'

'Coyotes did come into the camp,' agreed Martha. 'Clem Crenshaw told me that he'd seen them stealing food in broad daylight. At first, I just thought he was joshing, to make a little fun and cheer me up. But it was true. I had to deliver more dried meat, which he had to hang from a tree.'

'And you're saying coyotes took food and fed it to a fourteen-year-old girl?'

Gus nodded, 'It's the only conclusion I can come to.'

'I find that hard to believe,' said Doc Larkin.

'Then you better take a seat, Doc, because I've got something else to tell you.'

When Gus finished his story, explaining in detail his observations from the ridge and watching Chrissy closely surrounded by coyotes, the doctor said in astonishment, 'I have never heard of such a thing in my life.'

'That's a pity,' said Gus, 'because I was hoping you could offer an explanation.'

'Why me?' asked the doctor.

'You're an educated man.'

'Don't get education mixed up with knowledge,' said the doctor, 'it's a dangerous assumption.'

'Maybe the coyotes saw an innocent young girl in need and they took her into their family, to protect her. After all, in Luke 16, didn't the dogs lick the sores of Lazarus

71

when he was sick and in pain,' suggested Martha.

It did sound a bit far-fetched, but in defence of his wife, Gus added, 'I've seen young Chrissy around animals and she has a way. That Mayfield mule was ornery to his back teeth. He'd bitten Abe, yet he'd eat from Chrissy's hand.' Then he added, 'It was never something I was prepared to try. He was mean.'

'Well,' said Doc Larkin, 'this world is full of incredible things, so why not this one?'

Martha nodded.

Gus wasn't sure. It did offer a kind of answer, or maybe it was just one of those incredible things. An unexplained astonishment.

'All the same,' said the doctor. 'I think it best we keep this to ourselves. We don't want people to get the wrong idea. Could sound a bit peculiar.'

Both Martha and Gus nodded in agreement. It was definitely peculiar.

14

BOX OF BULLETS

Union Metallic Cartridge Company

People have a way of forgetting and maybe that's for the better. A family had been brutally killed and their home burnt to the ground, yet a child had somehow escaped and survived. It was a miracle, something to rejoice over and give praise to the Lord, said those devout Christians of whom there were many in Laramie. That Chrissy could not, or would not speak, added to the belief that she had been taken by savages and scared close to death. That she had not been physically touched during this ordeal was also a source of discussion, albeit in whispers. Some were sceptical, even when Doc Larkin made it public knowledge that Chrissy's virtue remained unharmed. Others responded by saying it was the hand of God protecting the innocent. But regardless of all the gossip and chatter, not once did the subject of coyotes ever get a mention. Doc Larkin, Gus, Martha and Henry said nothing, and why would they, when the occurrence of such an event was beyond comprehension?

Gus did take the opportunity early in the piece to talk to Chrissy, quietly, while sitting on the front porch. They were on their own and the sunlight was warm to the skin against the early chill. He didn't ask directly what she had seen that night. He just said that when she was ready to talk about it, he was ready to listen.

Chrissy just looked ahead, her voice silent and her face passive. It was as if she had withdrawn deep inside herself, so deep in fact, that she was no longer able to find her way out.

Henry too, had gone quiet and at times became lost in his own thoughts. He was protective of Chrissy, much like a big brother, and in turn she became close to him, often taking his hand as they sat side by side on the porch swing. Martha saw it as a bond of shared grieving that just had to take its course.

Gus returned to his duties and routines, but things were never as they had been for the Ward family. It was as if reason and joy had been sucked from their lives, never to return, and while his dyspepsia settled, it never really went away. His nights were often restless and when he did fall asleep he would have wild and vivid dreams of hooded men with flaming torches ransacking the Mayfield homestead. Each time he'd chase after them, but just as he was about to pull the hood from a perpetrator's head, he would wake with a start.

Martha was the one who seemed to cope the best. She filled every minute of every hour with work, and she did the same for Chrissy. Together they were like mother and daughter as Martha coached her in cooking, cleaning, washing, stitching, and every other household chore. Chrissy responded and participated willingly, yet, never a word was said in response. This was no deterrence to Martha, who chatted away providing both direction and encouragement.

Martha thought it best that Chrissy stay close to home and it was a wise decision. To most in town she was a curio and referred to as 'the Mayfield girl'. When she accompanied them to church she was stared at so intensely that Martha even considered that they stop going. It took words from the bible by Reverend Brown to convert her from such a thought, along with reserved seats to the rear near the christening font.

Henry did, however, take her out horse riding and it was clear that Chrissy had lost none of her skills. She rode with confidence and at times daring, riding both fast and hard. What also impressed Gus was the response of her mount. There was an unexplained affinity there, as if her horse was seeking not only to please her, but also to protect her. When Chrissy dismounted it placed itself close and twisted its head as if to keep an eye on her. It was odd, thought Gus, as he had ridden this same mount often and found it unresponsive, even a little ill-disposed. In hindsight of course, maybe it wasn't as odd as belonging to a pack of coyotes.

About a month later, Gus was out west and returning to Laramie when he picked up the road about a mile from the Mayfield property. Why he decided to go back and take another look, he couldn't say.

Nothing had changed. The ruins remained desolate and untouched. He walked his horse over to the home trough, dismounted and pulled on the pump to add to the water. As the horse drank he looked around to where he had seen Chrissy's footprints, then up towards the stockyard that was now empty. As he turned back, he glanced at the ground and there in a small pile were six spent cartridges. He squatted to take a close look before picking one up. It was clear that they had been ejected from a revolver to fall at the firer's feet. He turned an empty case over in his hand. It was devoid of any markings but he knew the calibre. It was .44. The only distinguishing feature was the centre-fired cap as opposed to a normal rim-fired pistol cartridge.

These new centre-fired rounds were becoming popular, especially for Colts that had been converted over from cap-and-ball ammunition. He examined each shell before putting the six of them in his top pocket.

Gus looked again towards the stockyard, the direction of Chrissy's footprint on that day he had seen it clearly by the trough. How had he missed finding these spent shells? Or were they recently discarded and left behind? He walked over to the fence, and there, just by a post, was the mark where a shot had split open the top rail. It was not recent, at least a month old. Was it a shot fired at Chrissy as she made her escape? Had all six shots been fired at her before the pistol was reloaded? It would seem so, concluded Gus.

The following day he strolled over to the general store and showed one of the spent cartridges to Ben Edmonds. 'Can you identify this?' he asked.

Ben took a close look. 'We sell similar,' he said. 'If it's UMC it could be one of ours.' Ben went to the shelves directly behind him and returned with a box of ammunition. The orange cover proclaimed *Union Metallic Cartridge Company (UMC) Fifty Central Fire .44 Calibre Ammunition* and below that it said, *For the new Colt Army Revolver.*

'Selling much?' asked Gus.

'They're getting popular. Good quality cases, can be reloaded.' Ben picked up the cartridge and ran his thumbnail over the centre cap. 'This one hasn't been reloaded. Fired from new. Where did you find it?'

Gus didn't want to say, so he just said, 'Found it yesterday. It was unfamiliar, so I thought I'd check.' He could tell immediately that Ben knew he had side-stepped his question.

Ben didn't press, he just said, 'I'll pay attention to who comes in for some of these, and I'll let you know.'

Gus half smiled, 'I'd appreciate that.'

15

A SHOOTING

The Stock Agent

'A shooting, down by The Red Blood, better come quick.' Deputy Joel Ferber was a little out of breath from hurrying back to the office to get Gus.

'Ivan there?' asked Gus as he grabbed his rig.

Joel confirmed he was with a quick nod as he sucked in a deep breath.

'Do we know who?'

'No.'

'Dead?' asked Gus as he tightened his gun belt.

Joel nodded again. 'Shot to the head.'

Gus pulled the buckle tight. 'Front or back?'

'Side. Left side. Above the ear.'

Gus took the office key from the rack and lifted his hat from the peg beside the door. 'Any witnesses?' he asked.

'None we've found. Plenty heard the shot. It was two cowpokes from the cattle yards who found him first.'

It took less than ten minutes for Ivan and Gus to stride out the half-mile to The Red Blood Saloon. A throng of sightseers were crowded around the street end of a narrow strip of land between the saloon and a dry goods store. Joel led the way, calling for a clear path as Gus followed. The land was used as a service lane for both the store and the saloon. A beer wagon was parked near the entrance, taking up most of the space. The horses had been unhooked and the tray was loaded with half a dozen barrels. Gus rapped one as he passed. It was empty.

Directly behind the wagon was the body, crumpled on the ground, half on its side, feet towards Gus, while one arm, the left, reached back with an empty hand. Deputy Ivan Davies was standing just a foot or two further on, closest to the head. He acknowledged their arrival.

'Familiar at all?' asked Gus.

'No,' said Ivan, 'not to me.'

Gus squatted and put his fingers to the neck. The skin was warm but there was no pulse. He lifted the head slightly to get a better view of the face, revealing a dark stain where the blood had soaked into the dirt. The dead man was freshly shaved and his moustache trimmed. He looked to be in his twenties. Gus lifted the upper lip and the teeth were all there and in good order. The clothing was neat and clean, except for where the body had fallen to the ground. Gus reached over and picked up the left hand. It was soft, the nails clean and trimmed. He looked down the length of the body to where the oak-tanned boots were clean and waxed. He stood, thought for a second before saying, 'Joel, get Hyrum, then let Doc Larkin know. Ivan, empty all of his pockets. Make sure you get everything.'

Both deputies acknowledged their instructions as Gus walked back to the crowd. All their eyes engaged him with interest. 'Anyone see what happened?'

No one responded.

'Where are the men who discovered the body?' he asked.

Two stepped forward together.

'Don't go anywhere. I need to speak to you about what you heard and found.'

Both said, 'Yes, Sheriff,' together.

'Anyone know this man?'

No one owned up if they did.

'Anybody see him earlier on? On the street. In a store. Talking to anyone?'

No response.

'If you become aware of anything that you think may help in identifying this man or the person or persons who did this, come and see me or one of the deputies.'

A sea of heads nodded.

Next, Gus motioned to the two men from the cattle yard who had found the body to step away from the crowd so he could talk to them. They had been less than fifty yards away when they heard the shot and went to investigate. They found the man where he had fallen, bleeding heavily from the wound to the head. From all visible signs, he was dead.

'He didn't say a word, then?' asked Gus.

The cowpokes confirmed that he didn't.

'See anyone close by? Running off?'

No, they hadn't.

Gus took their names and details of where they could be found before shaking the hand of each man. 'If you think of anything else, let me know.'

Gus returned to the body and began to examine the contents from the dead man's pockets that Ivan had retrieved. His name was Davitt Limborg. It said so on his Sons of Temperance card where he had pledged to abstain from the evil of alcohol for life, some four years earlier on the first of November 1866. Gus wondered if he had lapsed and was looking for a drink. If he was, he'd lapsed badly, as it was still early in the day. Other items included a nickel-plated pocket watch made in Switzerland, a cloth pocket purse containing five dollars in change, a return rail ticket back to Cheyenne, a handkerchief, and a small notebook with a pencil that slotted into the spine. On the leather cover were the initials CLA. Inside were printed blue-lined columns with letters and numbers. None of which meant anything to Gus. He flicked through the pages and only about a quarter of the book had been used. He looked at the cover again and guessed that the C stood for Cheyenne, but had no idea what the letters L A stood for. He waited with the body until the undertaker arrived. Before leaving, he reminded Ivan to pace out the distances from the end of each corner of the saloon and to draw up a diagram in his field notebook to accurately place the location of the body. He then went off to find and advise Mayor O'Brien and Judge Morgan.

He couldn't find either, but left word with each clerk to pass on the time of his calling, with instructions that there had been a shooting resulting in death, and that he would return later.

From there, Gus went to the telegraph office and sent the following telegram to Sheriff Laird at Cheyenne – *Shooting in Laramie this day, Davitt Limborg killed with wound to head, identified by temperance card, believed to be a citizen of Cheyenne. If known, please advise kin and inform me of reason for being in Laramie. Sheriff August Ward.*

Less than four hours later, he was advised of an incoming telegram and returned to the telegraph office. It was from Sheriff Laird – *Can confirm Limborg is a Cheyenne citizen. Kin advised and shocked at state of affairs. In Laramie on employment with CLA.*

Gus said to the telegraph clerk, 'Do you know what CLA stands for?'

The clerk looked at the telegram. 'Don't know,' he said, and showed it to the junior clerk; he didn't know either.

'Better ask,' said Gus. 'Will you give me another form?'

The man waiting behind Gus said, 'Cheyenne Livestock Agency. CLA. Here it's the LLA for Laramie Livestock Agency, but everybody just says the livestock agent.'

'Of course,' said Gus, sliding the telegram form back towards the clerk. 'You work for the CLA?' he asked the informer.

'No, I just raise hogs and sell them through the agent here. But I've sold some to the CLA when I can get a better price. Not supposed to. Supposed to keep to your district, but there's no law against it.'

'Obliged,' said Gus as he tipped his hat before leaving to speak to Larry Earnshaw, the Laramie livestock agent.

16

GUT

The Mayfield Stock

'I heard there had been a shooting. But Davitt! I didn't even know he was in town,' said Larry.

'Well, it seems he was here on business with the Cheyenne Livestock Agency. Do you know what that business could have been?' asked Gus.

'No, I don't. If it was a market day, it'd be my guess he was here to see the condition and prices of stock going under the hammer. But it's not a market day.'

Gus handed Larry the small book with the initials CLA on the cover. 'Does this mean anything?'

Larry seemed distracted as he thumbed through the pages and kept going back to the start before he finally said, 'Prices, stock type and numbers, that's all.'

'So, nothing surprising or suspicious?'

'No, no more than this.' Larry dropped a similar notebook with the initials LLA on to the desk. 'That's mine,' he said.

Gus picked up both notebooks from the desk and thumbed through each. They did look similar, but he had no idea of the significance of the contents of either.

82

'I heard it was just a stray shot,' said Larry.

'Who'd you hear that from?' said Gus as he finished looking at Larry's book and handed it back to him.

'Just street talk.'

Gus shrugged, 'Maybe,' he said and pulled himself out of the chair to stand. 'Would Davitt Limborg have had any business to do at the saloon?'

'He was a temperance man,' said Larry.

'Never lapsed?'

'Doubt it. Davitt was proud of his abstinence. He said drinking got in the way of work, and he liked to work. He was an ambitious man.'

There was something else Gus wanted to ask Larry but the comment on being ambitious side-tracked him, so he turned to leave, just to have it come to him. 'Has all the Mayfield stock been sold yet?'

Larry nodded.

'Get a good price?'

'OK for a quick and convenient sale. All sold as one lot. The proceeds have gone across to the judge. It will go to young Chrissy when the estate is settled.'

Gus took one step towards the door, paused, turned and asked, 'Did Rufus Cole end up purchasing any?'

Larry looked a little awkward as he said hesitantly, 'Yes.'

'How many?' quizzed Gus.

Larry was slow in answering before he said, 'The lot. He's building up a nice holding.'

'And where's he holding them, then?' asked Gus.

'West.'

'Where west?'

'He has property not far from the Mayfield land. Purchased it not long ago from one of the settlers who decided to move on. Meant he didn't have to move the stock far at all.'

Gus raised an eyebrow slightly. 'How close to the Mayfield property?'

Larry paused before replying. 'Just a little south-west. He said he might be interested in purchasing the Mayfield property if the price is right.'

'How long ago did he purchase his land?'

'Few months, I guess.'

'Didn't know that,' said Gus, almost as a whisper.

When Gus caught up with Doc Larkin, he was writing up his report on the examination of Davitt Limborg's body. 'Does the wound tell you anything?' he asked.

'Not a lot. Fatal. Almost instant death.'

Gus asked, 'Deliberate or a stray shot?'

'Can't tell. No powder burns to hair or skin to observe, and no smell of burnt hair,' said Doc Larkin. 'So, the muzzle would have been back some. It could be a stray shot. Have you any idea where such a shot could come from?'

'Nowhere from where I could see,' said Gus. 'The location of the body was between two buildings. Just walls both sides of where he was found, and no windows.'

'Enemies?' asked Doc Larkin.

'He was a stock agent from Cheyenne,' said Gus. 'Who'd want to kill a stock agent?'

'So, what was he doing down at The Red Blood Saloon?' asked the doctor casually.

'I don't think he was doing anything at The Red Blood. He's a—' Gus corrected himself. 'He was a temperance man. Had a return ticket to Cheyenne and wasn't too far from the stockyards. Two cowpokes found him just after the shot was fired. He may have just been taking a short-cut into town.'

'Anything taken from him? Money?'

'Seems not,' said Gus.

'So, no theories?' asked the doctor.

'None. What about you?'

'Nothing from the examination. Just one shot to the head followed by almost instantaneous death.'

'Who'd want to shoot dead a stock agent?' reflected Gus.

'Who'd want to shoot dead any man?' responded Doc Larkin.

'Where do you want me to start?' said Gus. 'Vengeance, theft, greed, fear, jealously, hatred, drunkenness, anger, a dispute, personal gain, or just plain loco.'

'You left out one.'

'What's that?' asked Gus.

'To keep a secret,' said the doctor. 'Dead men don't talk.'

Gus returned to the mayor's office, but his clerk had yet to pass on his message, saying that Tuesdays were always busy down at the station. Gus said he'd try and catch him there.

He was to have better luck with the judge, who was in the mood for talking and offered a cup of coffee. Unfortunately, it was stewed and bitter. Gus informed him of what had transpired and the judge took notice and grunted his responses into his enamel cup.

In an act of self-discipline, Gus finished the last three mouthfuls of the burnt brew to signal that it was time for him to go. But he did raise one last question to the judge. 'Did you know that Rufus Cole is now running cattle?'

The judge said, 'Yes,' and added, 'he bought the Mayfield stock.'

'So I've been told,' said Gus without hiding his disquiet.

'The proceeds have been banked and are being held in trust if that's what you're concerned about.'

Gus shook his head. 'It's not.'

'But I can see something is bothering you.'

'Do you believe in your gut?' asked Gus. 'Does it some-times tell you when something isn't right?'

'I can't let it,' said the judge. 'I have to rely on the facts, just as you do, Gus.'

'I know, but sometimes—'

'Sometimes your gut gets irritable when certain names are mentioned, like Rufus Cole?'

'Pretty much.'

'I can understand that,' said the judge. 'But it's the same for a number of citizens in this town. It's the nature of the West. It draws in men with a past.'

17

PEOPLE

The Ward Family

Time began to weave its magic as only time can do, often unnoticed by those it touches most. With each new day, life went on, returning to the familiar routine. In the Ward household chores had to be done, while Gus and Henry dealt with the matters of law and order as they arose. Most were no more than misdemeanours – disputes between neighbours, petty stealing, drunkenness, children lighting a fire down near the livery, and as always, fighting outside the saloon on a Saturday pay-night. The two large unresolved events, however, remained – the Mayfield killings and the death of the Cheyenne stock agent. Like a pot that had come off the boil to simmer then cool, both occurrences were no longer such a hot topic of discussion.

Gus could never understand how people could wax and wane on matters of justice. Maybe he just didn't understand people. Surely, if justice wasn't done, and seen to be done, then it was justice denied. And just as surely, justice denied was injustice. Wasn't it?

He raised these concerns with both the mayor and the judge, albeit both casually and carefully, but neither seemed to share his concern. He also noticed that people seemed collectively to use words that toned down the actual details of both events. 'The Mayfield family had been killed in their beds,' was a common saying – not that they had been 'massacred or murdered'. It was as if each member had remained asleep, never to be awakened during the slaughter. Gus wondered at times if he was the only person who saw it as a savage and brutal execution.

Common acceptance also decreed that it was all the doings of savage Indians. Except that nothing had changed Gus's mind. Where was the evidence? Not one trace, from a search that had lasted one month when looking for the missing Mayfield daughter. The trouble was, however, if it was not renegade Cheyenne, then who? Gus could not bring himself to believe that anyone in his community could do such a thing. So, he looked outside and wondered if the Army had somehow been involved. They were at war with the Indians and on occasion attacked and killed women and children. Was it drunken soldiers? Yet the 2nd Cavalry at Fort Laramie had no such reputation, and besides, if he was chasing after drunken soldiers, he'd drawn a blank. The troops from the fort had been away from barracks and patrolling to the north at the time of the crime.

It was similar with Davitt Limborg. His killing had been described locally as 'a death', as if he had just fallen over and died. When his kin and employer confirmed that nothing had been stolen from his person and robbery was removed as the motive, it led to a wild rumour that he had killed himself, being a temperance man outside the doors of a saloon and tempted by the evil of drink.

'Where do these rumours come from?' Gus had asked

his deputies.

'The saloon, mostly,' said Ivan Davies. 'Some laugh about it and say he should have just come in and they would have bought him a drink.'

'The saloon wasn't even open at that time,' replied Gus. 'And he didn't shoot himself. He wasn't even carrying a gun.' His deputies were busy and engaged in other matters and Gus wasn't even sure they were listening, and that included his son.

Henry was back at work and keeping busy, but he didn't say much and often seemed lost in his thoughts. He was always punctual and his field book was always up to date, as were his reports. But there was now a distance between father and son.

'Just give him time,' Doc Larkin had counselled.

'Fine,' said Gus with a touch of derision. Seems time is the solution to all medical problems, he thought.

Both Henry's and Chrissy's silence did not make for a cheery household, and why should it be cheerful? thought Gus. What was there to be cheerful about? At least we are warm, fed and together, he concluded. Cheerful would have to wait, maybe forever.

Chrissy remained mute but in other ways she had settled into the Ward household as a productive member. To some who caught a glimpse when visiting, and wished to voice an opinion, she was referred to as 'that poor child' as if deficient in some way. Gus knew it was not so, and told Martha they were wrong and to pay no heed. Still, such talk angered Martha, who was protective of Chrissy as only a mother can be.

What Gus observed was an attentive and alert young woman. This first realization occurred when he wanted to add a pinch of salt to a slice of potato pie. Before he even opened his mouth, Chrissy somehow knew what he wanted, saw that it had not been placed on the table, got up, quickly fetched the small bowl of sea salt crystals and placed it before Gus.

'Thank you, Chrissy,' he said.

And Chrissy smiled ever so slightly in response.

It was a simple and small instance, but Gus turned it over and over in his mind and decided that Chrissy had not entirely withdrawn into herself, but that she was observing with clarity and responding. In fact, the conclusion that he drew was that Chrissy was functioning in every way as normal, except that she chose or was unable to speak. He told this to Martha who confirmed that she was indeed both bright and diligent – completing all chores and doing them exceptionally well. Martha also told Gus that in their own way they did communicate, it was just that they didn't use words.

Just one week later, Martha was using a wall calendar to date labels on jars of preserved fruit. Chrissy showed interest in the calendar and on the spur of the moment, Martha said, 'Chrissy, when is your fifteenth birthday?'

Chrissy turned the page to the next month and pointed to the 7th.

Martha put her arm around Chrissy and gave her a hug. 'Then we should celebrate and have a party.'

Chrissy's response was a little disconcerting, as she suddenly became agitated. Martha could see it in her eyes, which darted from side to side.

'Just us, Chrissy,' Martha quickly said. 'You, me, Henry and Gus. That's all. Nobody else. And you get to choose what we should put on the table.'

Chrissy relaxed a little and her eyes lit up.

'It's people, Gus,' Martha said. 'I think Chrissy is fearful of people. Fortunately, she has taken to us as her family, but not to others.'

'I don't blame her,' said Gus. 'I'm damned if I can figure people out either.'

Martha chastised Gus for using a cuss-word in the house and he immediately apologized. But she didn't say he was wrong about his assessment of people, just that he had been imprudent with his language indoors.

18

GUN PLAY

Marksmanship

Henry took Chrissy riding on the day of her birthday. It was what she wanted. She had not asked, at least not directly, but that didn't matter. Each in the family had now devised ways to communicate and in turn Chrissy would respond. Martha would have a running conversation that taught and encouraged, while Gus would smile in thanks for her attentiveness and Henry would say, as if talking to a young sister, 'Come on then, let's give the horses a run, but no racing till I say so.'

Chrissy would respond to each in her own way, but to Henry's offer to take her riding she would be at her most enthusiastic, bolting for her room so she could change into either her baggy cotton riding breeches or warmer buckskins that had once belonged to Henry when he was younger. This did raise an eyebrow from Martha, who asked Gus the question, should a young lady, now aged fifteen, be wearing pants and riding cross-saddle?

Gus felt the least qualified of all to answer such a question, but guessed that this is what fathers faced with daughters who took to doing the same things as boys. He reminded Martha that Chrissy had worked the property with her father and sister, which entailed fencing yards and mustering cattle. 'And through necessity,' he had said, 'when you muster, you've got to ride cross-saddle.'

'Did Grace ride cross-saddle?' Martha asked.

'I think they all did,' said Gus.

Martha frowned. 'Fanny and Agnes too?'

'I think so.' Gus could see that Martha was not convinced. 'If she goes back on to the land, she'll have to work cattle.'

Martha hadn't thought that far ahead. He could see it in her face. 'Don't worry,' he said. 'It will work itself out, she is just fifteen.' But as soon as he said the words, he knew that time was moving faster than they both realized. Grace had only been three years older than her younger sister, and only seventeen when she first met Henry.

Chrissy gave a wave as she passed through the kitchen like a whirlwind to get to Henry, who was now calling on her to hurry up if she wanted her 'birthday outing'.

The ground that Henry selected he knew well. It was almost flat, with just a slight incline down towards the river, and free from ruts and traps for a horse at full gallop. He pulled up with the words, 'This will be the start line.'

Chrissy drew up alongside. She knew what was coming and was itching to go.

'Not yet,' he said. 'You can only go on my command and I will give you a ten-second start, and then I am coming after you. And you are to pull up at the river.'

He waited.

Chrissy's eyes were fixed on the river ahead and awaiting his command.

'Got it?'

Chrissy nodded.

He ignored her gesture. 'I didn't hear. I said, have you

got that?'

Chrissy nodded again, this time enthusiastically to get her point across.

Henry looked away in silence.

Chrissy was getting annoyed and pulled her horse in close to reach across and tug at his sleeve.

He kept looking away. 'I didn't hear,' he said.

She tugged again, this time pulling Henry across in the saddle.

'If you don't tell me that you understand then best we head home,' he said.

Chrissy jerked at his sleeve wildly.

'Then tell,' he said.

An odd warm breeze that seemed to come out of nowhere brushed upon their faces to take the chill out of the air. It only lasted for a matter of seconds, like some tiny chinook wind that just swirled around the two of them. 'Yes, Henry, I understand,' she said quietly, then bolted her horse into a full gallop.

Henry was so surprised that this little game had actually elicited a response that he forgot to start counting to ten and had been left behind.

The wild ride to the river was exhilarating. The wind blasted their ears and the vibration of the pounding hoofs could be felt through every inch of their bodies. Chrissy leant forward, almost resting her cheek on the neck of her charger, as she felt the strength and power of the horse beneath her, while Henry pulled off his hat and flicked it back onto the rump of his horse. To watch these two skilled riders was to observe beauty in motion. They raced on towards the river with the grace and speed of a low-flying hawk.

Who won? It was close, very close, but Chrissy claimed victory and couldn't stop laughing, which caused Henry to smile. Her laugh was warm and familiar and for just a moment, it felt like Grace was with him again.

After watering the horses and checking each leg for any heat or swelling, Henry caught sight of a jack rabbit on the other side of the riverbank. He pulled his Winchester from the scabbard, bent down on one knee, took aim, and fired.

He missed.

Chrissy let out a snigger and shook her head slightly, as if to say, Not very good, Henry.

'Like to see you do better,' he said.

Chrissy extended both hands for the rifle. Henry hesitated, but only for a moment. She took the Winchester confidently, knelt, and pulled it into her shoulder with her head raised as she looked for a target.

Henry sighted one. An old dead branch from a twisted and knotted fir tree that hung down close to the river's edge. 'See that old branch, just right a little. I want you to shoot where it touches the ground.'

Chrissy nodded once and gently laid her cheek to the stock. She took aim by aligning the front and rear sights on the exact point that Henry had selected, then easing out her breath just a little, she focused on the foresight and squeezed the trigger.

The rifle fired and she missed.

'How sad,' said Henry in mock concern.

The shot had missed just to the left and was a little low, not unlike Henry's shot. This showed that the iron sights were not aligned to either Chrissy's or Henry's eye. This was not uncommon. Rifle sights needed to be adjusted for each individual so that the line of sight accurately reflected where the shot would fall. This was not a difficulty to fix but tools were required. The quick and popular solution was to aim off, but this required skill because the exact distance had to be estimated for both latitude and elevation if the intended mark was to be hit.

Chrissy pulled down on the lever and ejected the spent cartridge. She took up her position once again, resighted on the target and slowly shifted the aim to the right a little and up a little. Easing her breathing she paused, held steady, focused on the point of aim and fired.

The shot hit its mark.

Chrissy pulled down on the lever with one smooth action, resighted and fired quickly. The target was struck a second time. She continued to pull down, sight and fire, and struck the target again. Then once more. All four shots hit the mark.

Henry was impressed. He had been put to the test, so he pulled his Colt single-action Army from the holster, extended his arm, pulled back on the hammer, took aim and fired. With relief, he hit the same mark.

Chrissy squealed with delight and clapped her hands.

Henry put his pistol back into the holster, pride intact and feeling more than relieved with the result.

Chrissy grabbed his wrist and for a second or two he thought she was pleading for him to do it again. He had no intention of pressing his luck. It was time to quit, while ahead. But what he soon realized was that Chrissy wanted to take a shot herself. He mulled it over. Why not?

Henry withdrew the pistol. 'Ever fired a handgun before, Chrissy?'

She shook her head.

Second thoughts came to mind, but it was too late now so he dismissed them. Chrissy was not just safe around a rifle but skilled, he told himself. And she could handle a horse as well as he could. He placed it in her hand, the hammer still forward with the firing pin against the fired cartridge.

Chrissy's hand sagged a little as she adjusted to the weight.

'Grip firm,' he said, 'now extend your arm. Pretend the barrel of the pistol is your finger and point it to where you want to aim.'

Chrissy did as instructed and selected different targets each time she pointed the Colt.

Henry watched intently. 'Now pull the hammer all the way back. Try not to lift the barrel as you do.'

Chrissy pulled back on the hammer, it clicked and the cylinder rotated.

'Now look along your arm, over the top of the barrel to the foresight, aim just like you do with a rifle and squeeze the trigger.'

The Colt Army fired, kicking the muzzle up, but Chrissy held firm and lowered the barrel. The shot had gone high over the target.

'Don't worry,' said Henry. 'Pistols tend to shoot high, you just need to get used to it and compensate.'

The next shot was closer to the target, but still high. Her third shot was closer again, but also high. With her fourth shot, and concentrating hard, she hit the mark.

Henry took the Colt from Chrissy and she observed as he reloaded five rounds, leaving one chamber empty, which he aligned to the hammer. He went to put it back in his holster, but Chrissy was holding up a finger to indicate that she wanted one more turn.

'No, we've got to go,' he said.

'Please?' came the plea from Chrissy.

Henry relented; she had spoken again. He handed her the revolver.

Chrissy gripped the handgun, pulled back on the hammer, concentrated and began to fire all five shots with less than three seconds apart. The first and second missed, but not by much. It was the last three that impressed. All hit the target.

Henry commended her skill with a warm smile. Yet it was not her marksmanship that he thought about on the journey home. It was Chrissy, the younger sister of his beloved Grace, who had been found when all thought she was lost for good or dead. Could she possibly take her sister's place in his heart, he wondered?

19

SUPPLIES

The General Store

Henry waited until he and his mother were alone before passing on the news that Chrissy had spoken. Martha clasped her hands to her cheeks, saying, 'Thank the Lord,' and began to cry. 'Oh, Henry, that is such wonderful news, isn't it?'

Henry agreed and gave her a hug. He had not seen her this happy in such a long time.

Martha believed it was best not to press Chrissy to talk, but to let it happen in its own good time. Gus agreed, but did so while dwelling on the consequences that now lay before him. Could Chrissy tell him what had happened to her and her family?

Gus sought advice from Doc Larkin, who was most interested in the details and circumstances that had led to this significant event. In turn, he agreed with Martha, while taking some pride in his own advice by saying, 'Told you time heals, Gus. Best we just let it run its course and let Chrissy speak when she is happy to do so, but I want

99

you to tell me all that happens. I'm going to make notes. This is a most interesting study. I have since learnt that there are recorded incidents of young men who have not spoken a word since the end of the war. Their tongues just froze. Did you know that?'

Gus did not.

'Most interesting, most interesting, the workings of the human mind.'

'I just want to know what she saw on that night,' said Gus.

'I'm sure you do, and so do we all, but don't be impatient, Gus. Besides, she might not be able to tell you any more than it was Indians.'

'Maybe,' said Gus, but he didn't believe it.

The rediscovery of Chrissy's voice was seen by Martha as the mercy of God. Gus didn't offer an opinion on such provenance. His faith was hanging from the thinnest of threads, but he had never told Martha that he had lost his conviction. He was happy to support her in her faith, and maybe sometime in the future he would return to his. But for now, he'd ceased to believe in miracles. The war had taken care of that.

Martha regained confidence in Chrissy's ability to recover fully and set small goals to be achieved. One of these important milestones was for Chrissy to leave the house and accompany her to the General Store to purchase supplies. The approach taken by Martha was gradual and the first step in this progression was for Chrissy to make out the list of required provisions. This she did with keenness and diligence. The written list, in pencil upon the kitchen notepad, was neatly lettered and the words spelt correctly.

When Martha finally asked Chrissy if she might like to come along and drive the buckboard for her, the response was at best tepid, but Martha persisted by getting her to harness the horse. Once done, she asked again, 'Chrissy, would you drive for me?' The horse snorted as if to ask the same question and the urge to hold those reins was too great. Chrissy relented.

The list of supplies was not extensive so the trip would-n't take long, and they would go no further than the store, returning home to place the provisions in the pantry before commencing baking. Chrissy climbed up onto the seat next to Martha and with a flick of the reins, they were off.

The ride into town was uneventful, but a little chilly. They had not rugged up sufficiently. Nevertheless, this was really no more than an inconvenience. On arrival, the store was busy with the hustle and bustle of customers. They waited in line, Chrissy now seeming a little unsettled until she became enticed by the large table festooned with fabrics at the back of the shop. From there she saw the boots, hats and coloured horse blankets on the back wall. Martha couldn't see Chrissy as she was obscured by bolts of cloth standing upright on a row of pegs behind the table, but she knew where she was.

As Martha was attending to her order and crossing off each item from the list, customers came and went, purchasing items, be they cooking pans or lamp oil or nutmeg, cloves, toffee or even a rolling pin. When a man stood beside her and ordered one hundred rounds of .44 ammunition, Martha paid little attention.

Ben Edmonds served the customer and asked, 'Rifle or pistol?'

'Army Colt, centre fired,' came the response.

Ben went to the shelves directly behind him and returned with two boxes and laid them upon the counter. 'Best quality,' he said. 'UMC for Colt's new Army revolver.

Says so on the package.'

The man looked down at the yellow label and said, 'That's them,' paid and left.

When Martha finished up marking off all her items, she called to Chrissy that it was time to go.

Chrissy did not respond.

Martha collected her change and called Chrissy again, asking her to help with the wicker basket and hessian sack now full of wares.

Still there was no response from Chrissy.

Martha was a little annoyed and went looking for Chrissy, while struggling to handle the supplies. What she found behind the fabrics near the horse blankets was a shock. Chrissy was crouched down low, eyes wide, and trembling like a hurt animal.

Martha dropped her load and the sack spilt as she embraced Chrissy with all her might. 'What is it, Chrissy, what is it?'

It was as if Chrissy wanted to tell her, to speak, but the words just wouldn't come out, just an odd stuttering yowl, not unlike a coyote pup.

Those in the shop now started to cluster around, gawking.

Martha was becoming frantic. 'Come, come, Chrissy, let's go, let's go home, now.'

And as they made for the door, she heard a voice behind her say, 'The poor Mayfield girl has embarrassed herself.'

Martha looked back to see the wet trail upon the floor behind Chrissy.

Martha was most troubled with this event and put Chrissy to bed. She said to Gus it mystified her how she could be doing so well one minute, only to return to a situation that was worse than when she had come to them. Henry went and got Doc Larkin who examined Chrissy. He prescribed Mrs Winslow's Soothing Syrup, which he said would remove any nervousness and allow her to rest.

Later that evening, Ben Edmonds dropped by with some of the groceries that had spilt from Martha's carry sack. Gus thanked Ben for his courtesy and walked him outside to say farewell.

Just as Ben put his foot on the wheel hub of his buckboard to climb up, he said. 'Nearly forgot, Gus. I sold two boxes of UMC .44 revolver cartridges today.'

'Who to?' asked Gus.

'Calvin Moy,' said Ben.

Gus felt his stomach churn. 'When exactly?'

Ben shrugged, 'Can't remember exactly.'

'Could it have been around the time that Martha and Chrissy were in the store?'

Ben thought for a minute before saying, 'Yeah, I guess it was around that time.'

20

PROTECTION

Adoption

Neither Gus nor Martha could sleep that night, but for different reasons. Martha worried about the state of Chrissy, while Gus worried about what he might have stumbled upon. If the presence of Calvin Moy in the general store had resulted in the regression of Chrissy, maybe she had linked him to the killing of her family, and that was also a direct link to both his brother Aaron and his half-brother Rufus Cole.

The more Gus considered their implication, the more concerned he became. They were members of the community, and for all their faults could he honestly believe that his suspicions should extend to the murder of Abe and his family? And if it did, then what was their purpose? What would they have to gain? Sure, Cole had purchased the Mayfield stock, but he'd bid and his offer had been accepted. He had also given generously towards the funding of the search, when the three of them attended the funerals. Were these not acts of compassion? Was Gus just displaying his own personal prejudice? Anyway, how could he convince anyone of their personal involvement, let alone a court of law? Where was the evidence?

Chrissy remained in bed for the next two days, and only left her room on the urging of Henry to help him groom two horses, which he brought up to the house from the livery. It was a ploy, but it worked. On seeing Chrissy relax, Gus decided that should the opportunity arise, he would try and seek some answers from her.

It was nearly a week later that an occasion did come about. Martha asked Gus to read to Chrissy to help soothe her to sleep. She suggested the bible, which didn't much please Gus and besides, he couldn't think of a suitable text. Henry had moved out of his room to make way for Chrissy, and Martha had fancied it up a little. On a small shelf above the bed she had placed some of Henry's child-hood books, and one of these volumes was *Ivanhoe*.

'You'll enjoy this one, Chrissy, I know I did. It's called *Ivanhoe*.'

Chrissy looked despondent.

'It is the story of knights and maidens in the court of a king a long time ago.'

Still no response.

'And of course, it's about their horses.'

It worked; Chrissy's eyes flashed. With that Gus turned to the first chapter and began to read of beautiful hills and valleys, but when his eyes sighted the words *gallant outlaws* he stopped. There was no such thing, he thought. You either live within or outside the law – and if you live outside the law then there are consequences.

Chrissy was becoming restless. Gus glanced back at the page and decided to abandon the printed words and make up his own story. 'If these fine Englishmen share anything with us today,' he said as if reading carefully, 'it was the love of their horses.'

Chrissy cupped her hands upon the blankets as Gus continued with his made-up story of fast rides down craggy ranges, high jumps over walled fences, and the stamina of man's best friend. When he finished and as he was about to say good night, she sat up and kissed him on the cheek, which took Gus by surprise. He patted her arm in response. 'You know you will always be safe here, Chrissy, with Martha, Henry and myself, don't you?'

She nodded.

'And if you ever felt unsafe, you would tell us, wouldn't you, so we could protect you?'

Chrissy nodded, but it was a slow nod.

'You saw someone in the store, didn't you? Someone you need to be protected from?'

Her eyes darted from side to side, before she slowly and deliberately nodded again.

'Don't worry, Chrissy, we will protect you, I will protect you as if you were my own daughter. Do you understand?'

She nodded.

'But do you believe me?'

Chrissy reached up and hugged Gus around the neck, as he said, 'It is my promise to you, Chrissy. This family is your family now.'

When Gus spoke to Martha later that evening, it was to ask her if he should speak to the judge regarding the adoption of Chrissy.

'Isn't that what we've done?' she replied.

'Yes,' said Gus, 'it is, but not in the eyes of the law. She is considered a child without kin and having no legal guardian.'

'Aren't we now legally responsible?' asked Martha.

'No. By the law, Chrissy is like the Mayfield property,

liable to the judgement of the courts.'

'Which courts?' Martha was more than a little vexed.

'Well, in our district, it would be Judge Morgan's court.'

'What right has he to make such decisions?'

'The right of the law. Chrissy is lucky she has you as her second mother. That is not always the case for all children who lose their family. The law is therefore necessary.'

Martha softened. 'Then best we make it lawful, Gus.'

'I think so too. She needs a family to protect her.'

When Gus spoke to the judge, he seemed in general agreement with the proposal, but hesitated.

'You have concerns?' asked Gus.

'None on your fitness as a family to care for Chrissy. Your two families were to be joined on the wedding of Henry to Grace. If ever sensibility should dictate that on the loss of her family, Chrissy should be put in care of the Ward family, then good reason has prevailed. But complications, as always, arise.'

'What complications?' asked Gus.

'Firstly, as Chrissy is over the age of fourteen years, she must consent to the adoption.'

'That's no obstacle,' said Gus.

'Has she has told you that she is willing to be legally adopted into your family, then?'

Gus hesitated.

'And I mean, told you,' said the judge, 'not just nodded her head. Because that is what she has to tell me as both a witness and as the authority for adoption.'

'She must tell you?' questioned Gus.

The judge got up and went to the bookcase besides the gun rack and pulled down a law book. He flicked through the pages, stopped, and read. 'Section 3 of the Adoption of Children Act. If the child be of the age of fourteen years or upwards, the adoption shall not be made without their consent.'

'And you want to hear her consent?'

'Not want, Gus, need. I need to hear, especially under the circumstances.'

Gus was a little puzzled. 'Under what circumstances, precisely?'

The judge leant forward a little towards Gus. 'That is the second complication. Chrissy is the last surviving Mayfield and her family property has a value.'

'Meaning?' asked Gus.

'I don't know how else to say it, Gus, but it has to be said.' The judge drew in a sharp breath. 'You don't want to leave yourself open to any allegation that you are seeking personal gain out of any such adoption. Especially as you are the law in Laramie.'

Gus couldn't believe what the judge had just said. 'Do you think Martha and myself are seeking personal gain out of adopting young Chrissy into the family?'

'No,' said the judge, 'I don't. But that doesn't stop rumour and spiteful talk. I'm only telling you this to protect you.'

'I would hope that no such false gossip would come to pass,' said Gus.

'So would I, but if I know people, which I do, some tattle is bound to occur. I've already been approached with an offer to purchase the Mayfield land. A pretty persuasive offer that would see the money paid into the trust along with the cattle money already held. And where money is involved, we need to be careful, and being careful is following the letter of the law. And what complicates all of this even further, is Chrissy remaining mute.'

Gus was now feeling a little light-headed. He had not expected any complications at the start of this meeting, but now they seemed to be everywhere. His mind began to spin with aspects of the law, community gossip, his reputation and possible sale of the Mayfield property. 'I see,' said Gus with a sense of despondency, 'and I thought it would be a mere formality.' Gus slowly got to his feet. 'I'll have to talk to Martha. She will be disappointed.'

'Don't lose hope, Gus. I know that Chrissy is being well cared for and I have no intention of changing that situation. She is best where she is and maybe she just needs a little time to get back to being herself.'

'Doc Larkin says the same thing,' said Gus in consolation.

'There, if a medical man says it is so, so should it be.' The judge was trying to be a little jovial.

Gus put his hat on to leave, but as he was about to depart, he said, 'Just out of interest. Who made the offer on the Mayfield property?'

'Rufus Cole,' said Judge Morgan. 'He wants to run his cattle on it, which now includes the Mayfield livestock. It all makes perfect sense to me.'

'Rufus Cole?' Gus felt his stomach churn and the burning of dyspepsia rise to his throat. 'Rufus Cole wants to purchase the Mayfield property?'

21

MOTHER NATURE

The Right Solution

When Gus spoke to Martha about his conversation with Judge Morgan, he left out most of the detail as he didn't want to dash hopes or worry her. He preferred to say that certain aspects of the law had to be met and that the law moves slowly. 'It has to get things right,' he said, so they just had to wait a little while. 'Just like we need to wait for Chrissy to find her voice again,' Gus added.

Martha was both disappointed and confused, but said nothing. She trusted Gus, as he knew the law – she didn't. Instead, she would turn to prayer and that was sure to work, she told herself.

Gus was much more open with Henry. He had to be. He now needed his help. 'We have to look after Chrissy,' were his opening words. 'She took fright the other day.'

'I know, Ma said it was being around people and it was her fault for making Chrissy go with her,' said Henry.

'Chrissy may be a little anxious around people,' said Gus, 'but I don't believe that was the reason why she took fright in the store. I think Chrissy saw someone that she recognized.'

Henry eyes narrowed. 'What do you mean, recognized? How?'

Gus knew that he had to be careful how he voiced his suspicions, but it was going to be difficult. 'I think she saw one of the men who came to kill her and her family, and it sent her into a state of fright again. A very severe fright.'

'Do you know who?' asked Henry, but before Gus could answer, he said, 'We should bring him in.'

Gus spoke slowly and softly. 'I don't have the evidence to bring anyone in, Henry.'

'But if we question him, then—' Henry was getting a little frantic and it looked to Gus as if his son wanted to go and make an immediate arrest.

'Just think this through for a moment.' Gus reached over and placed his hand on his son's forearm. 'We have to be smart about this. Yes, I have my suspicions and I want justice to be served. But if I bring him in, he will deny any involvement, and all we would have done is alerted him and any accomplices also involved—'

'Who is it?' butted in Henry.

Gus paused a little before saying, 'Best I keep my suspicions to myself, just for the moment. But when it is time to move, I am going to need you.' Gus squeezed Henry's arm.

'So, it's not Cheyenne?' questioned Henry.

'No, I don't believe it was, even from the start.'

'Someone in this town?'

Gus nodded. 'But don't you worry about that for the time being. I want you to concentrate on Chrissy and look after her.'

Henry nodded willingly.

'In fact,' said Gus, 'we must all protect her, like she is a member of our family. You should shield her as if she is your little sister. Your mother sees Chrissy as a daughter, much the same way she saw Grace as her future daughter-in-law. And that's why Martha would like to legally adopt her.'

Henry's head jerked back and his mouth opened a little. 'Adopt?' It was said with wonder.

'Yes,' said Gus, somewhat surprised by his son's response.

'Then she would be my sister, legally, like.'

'Yes,' said Gus. 'In the eyes of the law, that's correct.'

'But—'

'But what?' asked Gus.

'I, I, was thinking different, like. Like, I've found myself becoming attached to her.'

'We all have.'

'Yes, but if she became my sister then I couldn't marry her.'

A look of wonder was now upon Gus's face. Not for a moment had he thought of such a prospect.

That evening Gus quietly raised with Martha what Henry had proposed. Her response was one of stunned silence, before saying, 'I don't know what to say.'

Gus had done a little more digesting of the proposition. 'Yes, it took me by surprise too, but on thinking about it, well—'

'But he can't substitute Chrissy for Grace,' said Martha.

'I don't know if that's what he's doing,' said Gus. 'I think he has developed a genuine affection for her and on reflection we should have noticed.'

'But she is so young.'

'She is fifteen, three years younger than Grace.'

'You aren't proposing that they marry next year, are

you?' It was said as if to exaggerate Gus's argument.

'No,' said Gus. 'I'm not proposing anything at all. I'm just saying, a fifteen-year-old can be legally married with parental approval, and at eighteen they are free to marry of their own volition. We just have to realize that Chrissy is fast becoming a woman.'

'Chrissy and Henry, it's a sur—' Martha looked down at the floor as if she was searching for something.

'It is a surprise,' conceded Gus, 'but these things happen. It happened with you and me.'

'I was older, much older.'

'You were seventeen.'

'But we married when I was older, much older.'

'Nineteen,' said Gus.

'Times were different then,' protested Martha.

'Times were better then, back in Vermont, worse here, now.'

'In what way, worse?' said Martha disbelievingly.

'For every woman in Wyoming, there are six men,' said Gus. 'When Grace accepted Henry's proposal to marry, he became one of the lucky few to find a wife. Henry knew that. Is it any wonder that he has become attracted to Chrissy? There is nobody else now or in his future.'

Martha wasn't disagreeing, she was just lost in her own thoughts.

'I say we just let Mother Nature find the right solution. She usually does,' said Gus. 'After all, she found it for you and me.'

22

SACK OF FLOUR

Departures

When Gus walked in on Martha she was in a dither. It wasn't like her. She also seemed to be a little disorganised and that wasn't like Martha either. By nature, she was a planner who considered, arranged and prepared. Now, however, she was halfway through a bake and had run out of flour. He watched as she did her best to scrape up what was left on the table top, but there wasn't nearly enough to finish. She needed sufficient pastry to top the last two pies and from what Gus could see, she'd be lucky to stretch it to one.

'You can't depend on anyone any more.' She wasn't looking at Gus as she spoke. 'I asked Henry to get me a sack of flour.'

Gus had never heard her cast blame before. 'Where is Henry now?' he asked.

'Out riding. He took Chrissy.'

Was that really the matter, wondered Gus? That Henry had enticed Chrissy away from helping Martha? 'Chrissy loves riding, it is her only outing. It was riding with Henry that led to her first words,' he reminded her.

He could see that his wife was in no mood to accept explanations. Something had upset her. She could wait for Henry to return, but by then it might be too late to get to the store. She could have gone herself, but of course she would have to 'smarten herself up', as she was fond of saying.

'I'll go,' said Henry.

'No need,' was the curt response.

There clearly was a need, or was the need to stay angry? But at who – Henry, Chrissy, the pies? Gus walked over and took her in his arms.

'I'm busy, Gus.'

'No, you're not,' he said.

'Am so.'

'Can't be.'

'Why can't I be?'

'You've run out of flour,' said Gus and he felt his wife sink into him.

'What are we going to do?' said Martha and it came out like a whimper.

He was about to say, I'm going to get you some more flour, but he knew that was the wrong answer, so he just shut up. It was a lesson he'd learnt after twenty-six years of marriage.

'Chrissy, our Henry, us, what are we going to do?'

Gus patted her back. 'It will all work out. It always does.'

'No, it doesn't, Gus. Not always. Sometimes it goes bad, really bad. You know this Saturday coming was to be the day that Henry and Grace were to be married?'

Gus didn't. It had been a date sometime in the future – a date forgotten out of necessity by Gus. He hugged his wife tight as if to protect her.

'No, that's all, just a sack of flour,' said Gus to Ben Edmonds at the store.

Ben, always the salesman, said, 'Ever seen one of these before?' He placed a strange-looking device on the counter.

Gus had no idea what it was as he picked it up and examined the wire loops that extended from the handle.

'It's called a whisk. It's new from France. Just got 'em in.'

Gus was frowning as he asked, 'What does it do?'

'It takes the effort out of blending. Better than a spoon. Mixes quicker.'

'And that's good?' questioned Gus.

'The Frenchies think it is.'

'Do you use it in baking?' asked Gus.

'My word.' Ben picked up the utensil and waved it close to Gus's nose. 'You beat together ingredients when baking. Just the thing to use with flour.'

Gus pulled back a little and saw in the waving whisk an opportunity. 'Better give me one, then.' Only to enquire on the cost after he had bitten on Ben's dangling hook.

'Two dollars and fifty cents.'

It sounded expensive, but it was too late. Hopefully a French wire thing for beating up flour would cheer Martha up.

'Have you been over near the Mayfield property of late?' asked Ben in general conversation as he wrapped the whisk.

'No, why?'

'Had Fred Elwell come in and settle his account. Looked as grim as hell. Says he's heading back East.'

The shape of the whisk was clearly outlined in its wrapping and it looked odd. Gus was regretting his purchase as he asked, 'Did he say why?'

'No, he was in no such disposition. I think he was angry,' said Ben.

'Over what?'

'Don't know, but that makes the third family to quit in as many months.'

'Third?'

'Yep, the Hoods and Batchfords have already left. Are you after any smoking tobacco or maybe cheroots? Got some Old Virginia in yesterday.'

Gus didn't answer as he picked up the sack of flour and his gift for Martha. In fact, he didn't hear the question, he was deep in thought. 'The Elwell, Hood and Batchford families have all quit!' he mumbled to himself. Three families in three months. Why would they possibly do that, after all the effort and work required to establish their properties? It just didn't make sense. No sense at all.

23

UNDER A ROCK

Bev and Her Boy

Early the following morning, Gus asked Ivan if he knew that the Elwell family had quit to go back East.

He didn't. 'I know the Batchfords and the Hoods sold up and went back East a month or so ago,' he said. 'With the Elwells that now makes three families.'

'I know,' said Gus. 'Three in three months.'

'Who told you about the Elwells?' questioned his deputy.

'Ben Edmonds, down at the store.' Gus thought for a moment before asking, 'When did you last patrol out there?'

'Been a while,' said Ivan a little awkwardly.

'Should be every six to eight weeks,' said Gus.

'Yeah, I know, but we've been busy.'

'Not that busy.' The words came out with a little annoyance at what seemed to be an excuse.

Ivan responded by saying, 'We've been a bit short-handed of late.'

The words hit their mark and Gus got it. 'Right,' he said. Both Ivan and Joel had been covering for Henry. 'I'll take a ride out and check on the other properties.'

'I should go,' said Ivan quickly. 'It's my circuit.'

'No, no,' said Gus, 'he's my son that both you and Joel have been covering for, and I appreciate it. The least I can do is ride the western circuit. You hold the fort.' Gus looked around his desk. There was nothing there that couldn't wait. 'If I leave now, I'll be back tomorrow some-time, hopefully not too late.'

Gus picked up a mount from the livery and rode back home to tell Martha that he would be away for the night. She responded, as always, by packing his saddle-bags and pulling out his bedroll from under the linen shelf. When she kissed him on the cheek to say farewell, she squeezed his arm just a little tighter than she usually did. Gus responded with the words, 'I'd be lost without you, Martha Ward.'

'And I'd be lost without you, Sheriff August Ward, so you take care,' came her response, before she quietly said, 'If I was ever lost in this world, may it be with you.'

Gus kissed his wife on the lips and replied, 'As long as we have each other, we'll find our way.'

He was out at the Mayfield property by just after midday, where he stopped to water his horse from the home trough. As he stood, gazing at the ruins, he felt the urge to remove his hat and say, almost in prayer, 'I'm trying to find out who did this and bring them to justice, Abe. Believe me, I'm trying.' As he went to put his hat on, he stopped to say also, 'And our family will protect your girl, you can depend on that.'

It was the noise of cattle that caught his attention as he was about to mount. He looked across to the top yard, which was congested with stock. The property was being used. Was it by the neighbours or had Rufus Cole laid claim by running his cattle, the Mayfield herd, back on the Mayfield property? He would need to check.

Gus rode north-west, first to check on the Hood homestead as it was closest. Even from afar the place looked abandoned. Inside it was stripped bare. Yet, when he opened the stockyard gate to ride across to the Elwell property, there were cattle tracks that could not have been much older than a day or two. This caused him to consider, was Cole using this property as well?

The Elwell homestead was like the Hood property, and so was the Batchford place. Each now silent and empty, which left Gus with a feeling of cold despair. He had never been a farmer and he'd never run cattle, but he knew only too well of the hardship associated with making a living off the land. Sit and listen to any settler family and they will tell you that the first, second and sometimes third winters were a knife-edge struggle to survive. It took fortitude not to give in and give up. Long, relentless hours of hardship were the rule and a decision to leave would squander that hard-won legacy. Yet all three families had well-established properties and seemed set.

What made it worse was that the Batchford homestead was well constructed and in good repair for the coming winter snows. All the yard fences were up and gated and the ground behind the back of the barn was marked out with corner uprights in place for an addition. It told him the decision to leave had interrupted future plans – but why? Gus pulled his horse around to the east with the intention of riding till last light, now not much more than an hour away, then finding a suitable place to overnight. Tomorrow he'd talk to the neighbours on the other side of the Mayfield property and see what they had to say.

As the last rays of the sun came low over his shoulder, it highlighted a wisp of smoke from a freshly stoked fire. He stopped, a little apprehensive. To his knowledge there were no settlers this far out from Laramie, which meant it had to be from fellow travellers or Indians. A second dark curl slowly drifted into the sky, followed by another. He was of half a mind to just ride on, yet this smoke signal beckoned. It might have been on the outer limits of the district, but it was still his patch. He changed his mind and direction to go and take a look.

As Gus came over the far crest to look down the slope towards a wooded hollow, he was relieved and pleasantly surprised to see a small homestead. The sound of an axe splitting wood struck up, but he couldn't identify anyone in the fading light. Gus walked his horse on until he could make out a dark bulky figure chopping wood. Once closer, he saw it was a young man with an almost childlike face. On dismounting, Gus said, 'Doing a fine job, there.' He looked across at the large pile of split wood. 'Looks like you'll be well prepared for winter.

The young man looked up, stopped, but said nothing.

'Sheriff Ward from Laramie,' said Gus by way of introduction.

The young man just continued to stand and look.

'Gus Ward,' he said.

A voice from behind said, 'He can't speak. He's a mute boy, also a little hard of hearing. Not deficient, just no tongue and you need to speak up. It was the Lord's idea to have him born that way, not mine.'

Gus turned to see a smallish woman with a Winchester cradled in her arms. Her voice and stance showed her defiance and challenged her size or any impediments that had befallen her son. There was confidence and a strength of character on display. He took off his hat.

'We've not met. Sheriff Gus Ward,' he said.

'I heard. Can I see your star?'

Gus looked down and pulled his lapel back from his jacket where it had hidden his badge.

'I'm Bev Warren,' she said in response.

'Your boy is doing a grand job.'

'Yes, he is a worker, all right. Like his father.'

'Just the three of you out here?' asked Gus.

'Just the two. My husband is dead. Died at Shiloh.'

Gus paused before saying, 'Sorry to hear that, ma'am.'

'Me too. I could have done with him being around these last few years. He was from Tennessee. I'm guessing with that accent you were on the Yankee side?'

'I was, but I'm still sorry for your loss.'

'I was a Yankee too, an original from New England, but when you marry a man from the South you have to change your allegiance if you want to fit in, don't you?'

'Yes, you do,' agreed Gus, while wondering why she was armed. 'So where were you from, exactly?'

'Connecticut. Know it?'

'Know it well,' said Gus.

'And you?' she asked.

'Vermont,' said Gus, 'but now I'm all Wyoming.'

'Me too. Take a cannon to blow me off this property.'

'Glad to hear it,' said Gus. 'Because I see that some of your neighbours have left.'

'Some,' she mocked. 'All. Just us and the coyotes, now.'

'All,' repeated Gus. 'Why?'

The woman walked towards him and stopped just a pace away, with her hands tight around the rifle that was cocked and ready to fire. 'What do you mean, why? Are you telling me you don't know?'

Gus was being confronted by this pint-sized woman and it was a little intimidating. He wanted to step back and give himself some room, but to do that would look weak and concede ground. 'No, I don't know.'

He could see that she didn't believe him.

'I swear, I don't know,' he repeated.

'Well if you don't know, Sheriff, then where the hell have you been living – under a rock?'

24

JACK RABBIT STEW

And a Glass of Madeira

'Now you tell me this, Sheriff. Are you the father of the Ward boy who was going to marry Grace Mayfield?'

'It's Gus, and yes, that's right.'

'And Abe never said anything to you?'

'About what in particular?'

'About a land grab, that's what,' said Bev, her voice coarse as if she had spent the day shouting. 'And a cattle grab.' She thought for a moment. 'What do you call that? A property grab, I guess.'

Gus was standing just inside the door of the small homestead. 'Do you mind if I sit?' He pointed to the bench next to the table. 'I'd like to take some notes.'

'Go ahead. I'll light an extra lamp.'

Gus slid onto the seat, placing his hat beside him and pulling out his field notebook. 'Who's doing this grabbing?' he asked.

'I don't know them by name, we are yet to be introduced, but I'm expecting them any day now.'

'Why is that?'

'Because I'm the last one. Kick me out and they will have the whole valley to themselves. But when they do come, we'll be ready. When I caught sight of you, and it being just on last light, I thought, this is it. Then I saw there was only one of you.'

'How many were you expecting?'

'Abe said three. But I still had a bead on you, as soon as you came across the crest. I'm not going to be driven off my land or burnt alive in my bed like Abe and his family.'

Gus pushed his notebook away. 'Keep talking, I'll just listen. You tell me all you know, anyway you want, but don't leave anything out. Then I'll go so that you can fetch dinner.'

'Go where, Sheriff? There's nowhere to go. Even if my neighbours were still here it would be too far to travel at night. You can stay here.'

It was a good offer. 'I'd be obliged,' said Gus, 'but I don't want to intrude.'

'Intrude all you like. You're the law.' Bev propped her Winchester against the wall, close to the door. 'I'll talk while I get cooking or my boy will starve to death. Eats like a horse. You like jack rabbit stew? My boy loves it with boiled onions and potatoes. Got some of both. Each time a neighbour quits, we get the benefit. They have given us supplies they can't take with 'em. I haven't been near Laramie or Cheyenne in over six months and will be all right through winter. Still, a poor reward for losing your neighbours. And just when we were all doing so well. You like Madeira? Near on got a full bottle from Fred Elwell. I'd never tasted it before, but it's really good.'

Gus didn't even get to answer. Bev was speaking and

working at a rapid rate and jumping from subject to subject. A small green glass with a chip to the base was put before him and filled. As he put it to his lips, he smelt what was something like stewed fruit. When he sipped, it tasted delightfully sweet.

'Good, isn't it?'

Gus could do little more than nod in agreement as questions leapt to mind, but he decided to hold his tongue, lean back a little, enjoy the flavour of the Madeira and listen.

What transpired over that evening was what a preacher might call a revelation, or the discovery of a greater truth. Not just about what had been happening without any knowledge to him or his deputies, and therefore the mayor and judge, who relied on Gus to tell of such matters – but about his failure as a lawman to uncover such goings-on.

How had he been so blind?

Bev was now telling, without any prompting, where each link in a chain of events now fitted. Yet, had it not been for a puff of smoke, he might have ridden on past this woman and her son, and been none the wiser – or worse, left them to fend for themselves.

What else had he failed to see before him, now or in the past? Was he the only fool, not to realize he was the fool?

Between the sounds of pots upon the stove and the clank of cast-iron lids, Beverly Warren, a fellow New Englander, told of her life as a milliner in New York and the meeting of her future husband from Tennessee. 'Handsome as,' she said, 'and if you think I can talk, he could talk a leg off a chair. And so pretty. I don't know what it is about Southern men, but they can make an everyday word sound beautiful.' Then without a breath she would switch the topic to running stock and the price of cattle, and of an unexpected offer made to Abe to purchase his property lock, stock and barrel. 'Abe told me that he had laughed, as he was sure it was being said in jest. When one of them said to him that it was a business offer that he would be wise to accept, if he wanted to keep his family safe, well, he became concerned,' said Bev. 'He told me when Luke and me ran into Abe and Grace while moving cattle. We have to move our stock over Mayfield land to get to summer water. Abe rode up close and told me, away from Grace's hearing. He said he didn't want to concern me, but that I should watch out, just in case they came calling. He then told me that he was heading into Laramie in the next week or two to inform the sheriff. That was when he told me that Grace was marrying the sheriff's boy, Henry Ward.' Bev placed a bowl before Gus. 'Small world, isn't it? Let me fill your glass.'

Gus accepted the offer.

'When I heard that the Mayfield place had been burnt to the ground from Mavis Hood, and she said it was Cheyenne, or it could even be Lakota, I knew something was wrong. It couldn't be Lakota. I know Lakota. They aren't like Cheyenne. But I still thought that Abe had got to see you, and whoever was going around making threats had been dealt with.' Bev spooned the stew into Gus's bowl and it smelt good. 'I put a turnip in as well. Adds to the taste. But when Mavis was leaving, she was real upset and told me that they were told that if they didn't accept the offer put before them, they could expect the same as Abe and Fanny. I said, go see the sheriff, we'll fight them, whoever they are, and she said, it was no good talking to the sheriff.'

Bev paused just long enough for Gus to say, 'Why did she say it was no good talking to the sheriff?'

For the first time, Bev became quiet.

Gus looked at her, waiting.

'She said, if the sheriff couldn't protect his own future in-laws, how was he possibly going to save us? You want another serve, Gus?' said Bev.

Gus just shook his head. His appetite had deserted him, and in the silence a lone coyote called off in the distance.

25

THE LAW

The Livestock Agent

It had been a long ride back to Laramie, but it wasn't the distance or time in the saddle that made it lengthy. Gus was accustomed to saddle time. It was having to keep company with his own thoughts – thoughts of regret and failure that he couldn't escape. When he rode into town he went straight to the livestock agency to see Larry Earnshaw. 'We need to talk,' he said, without any greeting.

'Is it about Davitt?'

Gus was about to say, no, it's about Rufus Cole and the Moy brothers grabbing cattle and land, but he paused. The last twenty-four hours had alerted him to the need to listen. Davitt Limborg had been shot outside Cole's saloon. Was it another link that he had missed? Instead, he said, 'You tell me.'

Larry started to squirm in his seat. 'Davitt was coming to see me. I didn't know when precisely, only that he was coming to see me.'

Gus had to suppress the words, What the hell, spilling

129

from his lips. However, it was as if the stock agent was trying to get something off his chest. Was this a confession? Gus retained his offhand tone as he asked, 'See you about what?'

'Livestock sales.'

'And?'

Larry started to stutter his words. 'The, the, the—' He stopped, all the while avoiding eye contact.

Gus could feel himself getting angry. 'Spit it out, Larry. I don't have all day.'

'The Army at Fort Cheyenne signed a contract for the supply of horses and beef with the Cheyenne Livestock Agency.' He was talking rapidly. 'Big contract and the CLA was unable to meet demand, so Davitt came to me to purchase stock from the Laramie Livestock Agency.' Larry licked his lips nervously.

'And?'

'And, Davitt showed me the commercial contract signed between the Army and the CLA, and I showed it to Rufus Cole.'

Gus didn't understand the significance of Cole seeing the contract. 'So?'

'He got to see quantities and type of stock required and the prices they were willing to pay, which was above market price.'

'Why would the Army pay above market price?'

'Because they wanted certainty of supply and were willing to price any other buyers out of the market to get it.'

That made sense, thought Gus. 'Then what?'

'Rufus knew that the settlers out to the west could meet that supply, and that they stood to make a lot of money. And it was easy for them to get quality stock to market. They only had to drive them to the railhead here, then they could be freighted to Cheyenne in a day.'

'And Cole wanted some of that action?' said Gus.

'No,' said Larry.

'No?' questioned Gus.

'No, he didn't want some of the action, he wanted all of the action.'

'You showed Cole how he could make a lot of money fast?' said Gus to clarify that he had got it right.

Larry's body rocked in the chair as if agreeing. 'Not just a lot of money, but a fortune.'

'So where did Davitt Limborg fit into this?'

'It was a CLA contract but the livestock were going to be supplied by the LLA. The two agencies are supposed to work independently of each other. It stops market distortion, so we both had to hide that fact.'

Gus now understood. 'You were in collusion with each other and Cole.'

'Yes.'

'And you were both receiving a commission from Cole?'

'Yes, but Davitt didn't know it was from Cole. Not at first. He only found out later. I took the first few payments over to him personally, and he thought it had come from the settlers, then—'

'Then?'

'Then, somehow he found out that Cole was involved and he wanted more money, a bigger cut.'

'And?'

'And I told Rufus, and he said that if he wanted more money, it would have to come from my share.' Larry had sunk down in his chair, his shoulders hunched forward, his hands in his lap. 'It's all my fault. I asked Rufus to speak to Davitt just to hear him out.' He sucked in a quivering breath. 'I should never have shown Rufus the contract. I should have just kept this between Davitt and myself. We could have made just as much money, buying direct from the settlers.'

'So why did you show the contract to Cole?'

Larry was reluctant to answer. Finally, he said, 'We didn't have the initial capital for the first purchase of stock. We would need to borrow. Take out a loan.'

'Was that a problem?'

'The bank wouldn't lend to us once they knew that we wanted to purchase stock. It would be a conflict of interest as employees of the agencies. Besides. . . .'

'Besides what?' asked Gus.

Larry's head waved about before he said, 'I get lonely and I just wanted a little female companionship, that's all.'

Gus was confused, the conversation having taken a completely different turn, but he said nothing.

Larry continued, 'And you have to be invited to meet the girls at The Blood. And this was the only way I could get an invite. I had to do something of benefit to Rufus.'

Gus thought for a moment before asking, 'So in return, you got the girls for free?'

'No, I still had to pay, but it was worth it.'

Gus had to stop himself from shaking his head. 'How was it worth it?'

'I had the money to pay for them from the commission Rufus was paying me.'

It was twisted logic, thought Gus, but somehow Larry had convinced himself that it was a good deal. 'So who shot Davitt Limborg? Was it Cole?' asked Gus.

'I think it was one of the Moy brothers, but Rufus sent word that he wanted to talk to Davitt, to make sure everything was all right with the deal we had. Davitt wrote to me and said he would see me after he had met with Rufus.'

'He was lured to his death.' It was said as a statement of

fact from Gus, not an accusation.

Larry began to weep. It was a pitiful sight. He had confessed, but Gus couldn't offer him redemption. Greed and desire had begat murder and more.

'What do you know about Cole driving settlers off their land?'

'I sort of suspected.'

'Just suspected?'

'I have no proof, but Rufus wanted their land, all of it. And when he wants something, no one can stop him, he'll do whatever it takes.'

'Including the murder of the Mayfield family?' questioned Gus.

Larry's head jerked upright. 'Rufus said it was Cheyenne renegades.'

'So, you asked him?'

'Yes.'

Gus shook his head. 'You had your suspicions and he told you what you wanted to hear, didn't he?'

'I swear, I didn't know. I still don't. Others say it was Cheyenne as well. It could have been.'

Gus leant across the desk. 'Look at me,' he said.

Larry looked up with tears streaks running down his cheeks.

Gus felt no mercy. 'You and I know it wasn't Cheyenne.' He had to check himself from grabbing Larry by the collar of his jacket and pulling him out of his chair. 'We both know it was Cole and the Moy brothers, don't we?'

Larry was silent.

'Don't we?' yelled Gus.

'Yes,' he finally whispered.

'You and I both carry a stain upon our souls. Yours is of avarice and mine is of stupidity. We are both guilty and while we can't put things back as they were, at least we can put them straight.'

'How?' asked Larry.

'By justice, but it will be a justice delivered in a way that fits the sin, and you are going to help me. Right?'

Larry's eyes darted from side to side.

'Right?' repeated Gus and his tone was severe.

Larry swallowed hard. 'How?'

'We are going to get rid of Cole and his half-brothers.'

'How?'

'You are going to set the trap and I am going to kill all three.'

'I couldn't, I would be an accessory to murder.' Larry looked scared.

'You already are, but I'm willing to keep your secret. You can trust me, but you can't trust Cole. He has more than the Army contract to hold over you and he will never let you go. He's already killed one stock agent, what's one more? But this way, my way, you get to start over again.'

'But, but—' Larry was stumbling over his words. 'You can't kill, not like this, in cold blood or revenge, you are the law.'

'Yes, I am, and I'm going to administer the law as I see fit. There is no other way, and you are going to help me. You don't have a choice, so just nod your head so that I know we both understand each other.'

The livestock agent's eyes were wide and wet, mucus ran down from both nostrils to cross the upper lip of a half-open mouth, and as his chin quivered he nodded his head.

Consent had been given and the agreement sealed.

26

PAST BEING RIGHT

A Part to Play

Larry Earnshaw was on the edge of falling apart. Gus knew it and Larry knew it. His world of livestock auctions, sales, accounts, waistcoats and starched collars had been turned into a pretence, a façade. Instead, he'd become a grubby little crook with a desire for women and riches.

Am I any better? thought Gus. His was a crime of opportunity and desire, while mine is now one of premeditated murder. An eye for an eye. Gus held down one side of the rolled map as he said to Larry, 'Point out to me each of the properties that Cole now has control of. And start with the Mayfield land.'

'But he doesn't have control of the Mayfield property yet. He can't purchase until the court approves the sale. He's just running his stock on it.'

'On whose authority?'

'None.'

'So he's not paying rent?'

Larry shook his head.

'This is the Mayfield property, right?' Gus pointed to a patch of blue on the map.

'Yes.'

'What properties has he purchased?'

'The Elwell property here in pink. The Batchford property in yellow. The Hood property is this brown one.' Larry's finger moved to the other side of the Mayfield property. 'This was the Harmans' property here in green, the Randalls' in red, and the Kirkpatricks' in white.'

All the properties were clustered around the only source of all-year water that ran through the light blue patch of Mayfield land. Gus could now clearly see the importance of Abe's property to Cole's new empire. 'And this one to the north and further out to the west, is that Bev Warren's place?'

'Yes,' confirmed Larry. 'It's the smallest of them all. Rufus said he's in no hurry for that one. He said he'll get to it once he has secured the Mayfield property.'

'Is there any way we could get Cole to change his mind and make a move on the Warren property, now?'

'How?' asked Larry.

'You tell me? Is their stock good quality?'

'Sure, but Cole has plenty of good stock at the moment.'

'Is the property important geographically?' asked Gus.

'Not especially, not like the Mayfield property that has access to water over the hottest summers.'

Gus's finger tapped the map on the blue patch of the Mayfield property. 'There has to be a way,' he said under his breath.

Then he got it.

'Tell Cole that you heard from me that Chrissy Mayfield wants to sell her land to Bev Warren and her son, Luke.'

'Does she?' asked Larry.

Gus stood up to ease his back. 'Tell him that's what you heard from me.'

'I, I, I don't know if I could do that.'

Gus's mouth tightened. 'I'm not asking, I'm telling. So, what do you think Rufus Cole will do when he hears that?'

'He'll run her and her boy off, like he did to the others.'

'Will he move quickly?'

'Guess. He has in the past. He has to have the Mayfield property or all his plans fall apart.'

'Within a week? Would he move that quickly?'

'Guess.'

Gus fell silent, deep in thought, before saying, 'I may have to move out to the Warren property and wait him out. I just don't want to raise suspicion if I'm away from town for too long.'

'He only ever makes his visits to the settlers on a Sunday night,' said Larry. 'It is the one day that the saloon is closed and the three of them can get away. It gives them time to ride out in daylight and return the next day, early, without notice.'

'It's Wednesday – would he move this Sunday?'

'I don't know. He might, but I don't know.'

'I've got to know. I'll get one shot at this, that's all.'

'We shouldn't be doing this, it's not right.' Larry was squirming.

'Don't you go to water on me now, Larry. It's well past being right. We are going to do this, and we need to do it as soon as it can be done. We both have a part to play. Now, you get the word to Cole, and see if you can find out when he and his brothers will make their move.'

Larry went to speak, but Gus cut him off. 'Just do it or I'll come after you. I plan on killing three – one more won't matter.'

27

SETTING THE TRAP

Trust

Gus knew there was no going back. In his heart, he had already committed the crime and failed the foremost test of every lawman, to work only within the confines of the law. Yet a tranquillity seemed to come over him. He slept a sound sleep that night, one that had eluded him for months, and the burning in his chest seemed to have passed.

Larry Earnshaw on the other hand was a bundle of nerves. Just after Gus left his office and he was alone, he heard the last call whistle of the Central Pacific to Sacramento. He was of half a mind to make a bolt for it and run, but that required courage and right now that well was dry. His nerve was so near to breaking that in desperation he sought solace from a bottle of Wharton's whiskey kept in the bureau behind his desk. The first swig burnt as he swallowed, taking his breath away. But it was not enough, and each following mouthful was justified as necessary, as was his weakness for the company and comfort of a woman.

By the time he stepped onto the stairs of The Red Blood, leading to where the girls entertained those who had an invitation, he was inebriated to the point where fear had been replaced by a swagger.

'You're early,' said Demetri, the Russian who gave or denied access on the orders of Rufus Cole.

'With good reason. I need to speak to Mr Cole,' replied Larry.

'He's not here,' said Demetri.

'I'll wait.'

'You can wait downstairs unless you pay.'

'I'll pay, I'll pay,' he said with agitation. 'I always pay.'

Rufus Cole was standing directly behind Larry, who was unaware that he had been followed up the stairs. He tilted his head to Demetri to let the stock agent through as he stayed just a pace behind. 'You wanted to see me?' he said as they both stepped onto the landing.

Larry was startled, but the alcohol allowed him to regain composure quickly. 'Ah, Rufus, you surprised me.'

'You said you wanted to see me?'

'I got a visit from Sheriff Ward today.'

'What about?'

'About the Mayfield property.'

Cole took Larry by the arm and walked him away from three girls sitting on a red velveteen settee, so that they were out of earshot. 'What about the Mayfield property?'

'He says that the Mayfield girl wants to sell it to Beverly Warren and her son.'

'I thought the Mayfield girl had been struck dumb after the Indian attack?'

'Seems not.' Larry swayed a little.

'What else did he have to say?'

'Just that.'

'Why was he telling you?'

'He was asking about livestock.'

'What livestock?'

Larry had enough alcohol in his blood to respond confidently with a lie. 'He wanted to know if the sale of the land without livestock would be a benefit or a hindrance.'

'Huh,' snorted Cole in defiance. 'I own the Mayfield livestock. I paid for it fair and square.'

'Square, but not fair,' said Larry. 'I got it for you, and for a good price – a very good price. I told Judge Morgan that it was a fair price under the circumstances, but it wasn't. He accepted what I said because he trusts me. Do you trust me, Rufus?'

Rufus Cole trusted nobody, but Larry's lack of judgement in such matters was blind to that fact. Rufus Cole had lied, cheated and killed his way to where he was today. That he dressed in the finest wool, cotton and silk was no more than the disguise of a well-to-do businessman. Wearing the black hood of an executioner would have been far more fitting. 'Of course I trust you, Larry. That's why we are partners, but partners need to be discreet, just like you need to be when you come in here asking for me, when you're drunk.'

'I'm not drunk.'

'I can smell it on you.'

'I've just had a drink or two, that's all.'

'Why is that?'

The alcohol was now taking its full effect. The stock agent went to speak but missed his words, before saying, 'I, I, just needed it.'

'Don't you go soft on me, Larry, there is too much at stake. I've got another thousand head ready to be shipped and I don't want any mistakes.'

Larry stiffened. ''course not, you can depend on me.'

'Good,' said Cole, 'because if I can't, then I don't have any need for you. Have you got that?'

All of a sudden, Larry felt stone-cold sober. Gus had warned him that he couldn't trust Cole, that he had already killed one stock agent, so why not one more? The realization of the threat was like iced water upon his face.

'Got that?' repeated Rufus Cole, his voice sharp and piercing.

'Yes, yes, of course,' said Larry.

Rufus Cole smiled, 'Now off you go and have your fun.' The whole demeanour and tone of his voice had changed from threatening to soothing in the space of a few words. 'Lilly, come here and look after Mr Earnshaw. He is one of our special guests.'

The young woman responded with enthusiasm. 'It would be my delight, Mr Cole.'

'And his too, I'm sure,' said Rufus Cole as he smiled, turned and left.

'Drink, Mr Earnshaw?'

'No, not at the moment, thank you, Lilly. I'm feeling a little—' he paused, swaying slightly before saying, 'You'll have to excuse me, I need to go.'

28

BLOOD AND HEART

Eavesdropping

On hearing the news, the burning in Gus's chest was back in an instant. 'When did it happen?' he asked.

'Last night sometime,' said Deputy Ivan Davies.

'Where?'

'In his office. He was found this morning, early, by a clerk from the stockyards who went up to get him. He was late. Thursday is loading day and there was a shipment of cattle going out to Cheyenne.' Ivan flicked a page in his notebook before asking. 'Do you want to go see? Real messy.'

'No,' said Gus, 'just tell me how he did it.'

'At his desk, handgun to the mouth, took off the back of the skull. Hyrum says he'll remove the body and clean up, but only after you say so.'

'Tell him to go ahead. Who needs to be notified?'

'No kin in town. The clerk who found him said he has an uncle in Chicago who is also in the livestock trade. Seems it was the uncle that got Larry the job here in

Laramie. The clerk suggested that we send a telegram to the livestock agency in Cheyenne as they will know how to contact the uncle.'

'Go ahead and do that, will you?' said Gus.

Ivan put his hat on to leave.

'Just one thing,' said Gus. 'You said he was at his desk when he shot himself.'

'That's right.'

'Did he leave a note as to why he would commit suicide?'

'I looked, but nothing.'

'Check the drawers?'

'Yep, checked the top of the desk, the drawers, his wastepaper basket, the floor under the desk, even his pockets. Nothing.' Ivan lifted his hat, rubbed the top of his forehead as he said, 'Doing something like that. It just doesn't make sense, does it?'

'I'm not sure I know just what does make sense any more,' said Gus slowly.

Gus was now at an impasse. Had Larry set the trap for Rufus Cole? He had no idea, but his guess, his gut, said no, that the livestock agent had lost his nerve and taken flight to escape to the other side, rather than face Cole. But could he take the risk? What if he had? What if Cole was preparing to act and make his move against Bev and her son Luke, to drive them off their land? Or worse, kill them and burn the place to the ground like he had done to the Mayfield family?

Gus could feel the burning in his chest.

There was no choice. He couldn't take the chance. He would have to ride out on Sunday, and at the very least warn Beverly Warren that she and her son could be in imminent danger. He would stay the night and protect them, and if Cole and the Moy brothers turned up while he was there, then—

Gus paused his thoughts, his chest still burning.

Go on, he told himself. Then what?

He forced himself to answer, clearly and deliberately. Then he would kill them.

Somehow, this commitment calmed him. He knew he would have to face the consequences wherever they fell. Would a jury judge his actions as falling within the law even if he was to find the evidence that the three had murdered the Mayfield family?

Or if he lied and said it was in self-defence – would a jury believe him?

He didn't know, but he no longer cared, so why lie? If he was going to dispense justice his way, at least let it wear a shroud of truth by being honest with himself first and foremost.

On Friday, Gus reorganised the duty roster and advised both Ivan and Joel that he would be away on Sunday and return sometime after noon on Monday. He apologized for the inconvenience, saying that he needed to follow up on some missing district papers from the June 1 census. He knew that his deputies disliked anything to do with the national census, as they did not consider it to be law work, so they would be happy that someone else was looking after it.

On Saturday, he told Martha the same 'white' lie he had told his deputies. He then walked down to the office where Joel was on duty and attended to some overdue paperwork, before heading across to the livery stables. His intention had been to select and take a horse back home with him so that he could leave for the Warren property as soon as he had attended church with Martha. This plan was altered when one of the stable boys mentioned that he could bring a horse to his home on Sunday morning. 'I can do it before I deliver the others,' he said.

'Sure,' said Gus, knowing that the boy was chasing a tip, before asking, 'Where do you have to deliver the other horses?'

'The saloon,' said the boy. 'Just after lunch.'

Gus felt his back stiffen while he tried to say casually, 'How many?'

'Three of the best. Mr Cole likes fast horses.'

Gus returned home with a sense of both urgency and anticipation. He drew up a chair at the kitchen table and began to strip and clean his Winchester and his Colt revolver. He was deep in thought and wiping each individual round of ammunition with a soft cloth when Henry walked in and sat down.

'You want me to come with you?' his son asked.

'No,' said Gus, 'it's just census papers.'

'So Joel told me. And maybe a bit of hunting?' asked Henry, looking down to the row of .44 rifle ammunition that had now been polished bright.

'Yeah,' nodded Gus, 'maybe a jack rabbit or two.'

A silence followed. Gus kept polishing while Henry looked directly at his father. 'There are no lost or outstanding census papers, are there?'

Gus kept cleaning.

'I helped fill out the return sheets and took them down to be signed off by Judge Morgan, myself. They were all present and correct. He said I'd done a good job.'

Gus's deceit had been exposed by his own son. He picked up the next cartridge and wiped it carefully with the cotton cloth.

'And you're not hunting jack rabbits, you're going after something altogether different, aren't you?'

Gus wasn't game to look up at Henry in case his son saw the pretence upon his face.

'I want to come with you,' said Henry, his voice strong and calm.

'You can't,' said Gus.

'Why not?'

It was no good deceiving any more. 'It is something I have to do, and it is best left with me. I don't want you involved.'

'But I am involved. I'm your son. Grace was my betrothed. And now I have fallen in love with Chrissy. You can't untangle any of that. It is what it is, blood and heart.'

Gus felt an uncontrollable surge of love for his son. It rolled over his body like the warmth of a chinook wind as it sweeps down to escape the icy clutch of winter. It was like inhaling balmy spring air. His first and only child. The son his wife had presented to him twenty-three years ago, was now talking to him man to man, and telling his father of the ties that bind.

'Are you going to finish this once and for all?' Henry asked.

Gus looked up. 'Yes, one way or the other, once and for all.'

'Then I want to be beside you when you do, Dad.'

Gus looked at his boy with pride and bit on the edge of his lower lip before slowly saying, 'We will need to leave straight after the church service.'

'Where are we going?'

'West, then north to the Warren property, and we need to be there by last light. Check your rifle, handgun and ammunition, and be ready for bad company.'

'How many?'

'Three.'

'Who?'

'Rufus Cole, Aaron and Calvin Moy.'

Henry's eyes widened. 'You think they were—'

Gus cut in. 'Yes, but I can't prove it. That's why we have to wait for them to try and do it again. And when they do, I'm going to strike. No arrests.'

Concern etched Henry's features.

'I know,' said Gus, 'but it's no longer a matter of choice. All I want you to do is cover my back. You'll need a good mount. Best you go talk to the livery.'

'There are two good horses here, I've just taken Chrissy for a ride,' said Henry. 'I'll keep them overnight and we can use them.' Henry got up from the table. 'I'll get my guns.'

When Henry pushed back on his chair to stand, and the legs scraped against the floor, he thought he heard the scamper of feet from the other side of the kitchen door. But when he opened it, there was nobody there.

But there had been and now they were gone.

Chrissy had been listening, and the pristine hearing of a fifteen-year-old girl meant that she had heard everything. Every detail, and that included Henry's love for her and the names of Aaron and Calvin Moy.

29

THREE FINGERS

Smart

The decision to leave before the church service was made on the urging of Henry. His logic was sound. Why wait? They had a long ride ahead and the extra few hours would make it easier on the horses. However, for Gus there was now a missing piece to his original plan. He had wanted to go to church with Martha, to be close by her side as he silently sought forgiveness for future sins.

Henry obtained permission from his mother for them to leave straight after breakfast, and like his father he kept up the pretence with a lie. 'The earlier we leave, the sooner we'll be back,' he had said.

Martha wanted them back, and the two men in her life slipped away just before she and Chrissy made ready for the church service. With his departing kiss, Gus told his wife that a boy would come with a horse from the livery, and that she should tell him that it was no longer required but pay him a small gratuity for his service. Chrissy stood just off to one side as she cleared the plates from the breakfast table.

148

They were over fifteen miles out of town when Gus caught sight of a rider in the distance, over to their left, on the old wagon track. He expected that the traveller would overtake them, and probably turn north, as that was the direction of the old track. But the rider slowed, departed from the track and started to pace them for the next three or four miles until they were close to the Mayfield property.

Henry didn't pay much notice to the company until he put his water canteen to his lips and took a longer look. 'Arr, jeez,' he said and pulled up his horse.

'What is it?' asked Gus.

'It's Chrissy.'

'What?' Gus looked. 'Are you sure?'

'Yes, I know how she sits.' Henry pulled his horse around and started riding towards the figure that had come to a halt some three or four hundred yards away.

Gus followed and as he got closer, saw that it was indeed Chrissy.

Henry reached her first and opened the conversation with, 'Chrissy, what are you doing here? You have to go back.'

Chrissy sat silently looking at Henry as Gus arrived.

'Head back straight away, Chrissy,' continued Henry.

She shook her head defiantly. It was clear that she was not going anywhere.

'And where did you get that mount?' Henry was now showing his annoyance.

'It's the horse from the livery that I ordered,' said Gus.

'She'll have to go back,' said Henry.

'I agree,' said Gus, 'but not on her own. I don't want her running into any bad company coming this way. You'll have to go back with her, Henry.'

'But—'

149

'No other way,' said Gus, just as Chrissy called out, 'Yah,' and rode between the two of them and towards the crest that overlooked the Mayfield property.

Gus pulled his horse around, 'Come on, Henry, she's heading for the ruins of her old home.'

Chrissy rode at a full gallop, showing both style and ease, and neither Gus nor Henry were going to catch her. They slowed when the ruins of the homestead came into view, and by the time they did catch up she had dismounted and was watering her horse from the trough by the water pump.

Gus dismounted and led his horse over. As it drank, he took off his hat and leant over to put his hand on her shoulder. 'You ride well, Chrissy,' he said. 'I've seen men who think they are smart on a horse, but not as smart as you.' He then shook his head. 'Chrissy, you'll have to go back with Henry.'

Chrissy looked at Gus, glanced at Henry, then back to Gus, before quietly saying, 'I heard what you told Henry. I was listening at the door. I heard the names.'

Gus tried not to show any eagerness as he asked, 'Had you heard any of those names before?'

'Yes.'

'Which ones?'

'Aaron and Calvin.'

'Now, this is important, Chrissy. How many men were here on that night, can you remember?'

Chrissy looked over at Henry then back to Gus before holding up three fingers and saying, 'Three. There were three men. The one on top of me was Calvin, the one on top of Grace was Aaron.'

'Do you know what we are going to do, Chrissy?'

Chrissy nodded again.

'Do you want to come with us and identify the men who

did this?' Gus glanced at the ruins of the Mayfield home. 'Do you?'

'Yes,' she said, her voice firm. 'I want to go with you and Henry.'

30

FULL MOON

Coyote Call

They rode in silence, each with their thoughts, Chrissy close to Henry, and Henry close to Gus. They stopped every hour, briefly, to check their horses, but barely a word was said. As last light faded, a full moon rose early to cast its own pale light.

Gus knew they were close, but was unsure if this was the crest that looked down upon the Warren homestead, or the one after. The silhouette of the fir trees in the hollow looked familiar, but he expected to see the glow of an oil lamp, so he told himself it must be the next ridge on.

Just as he lowered his head a little, to better examine the ground underfoot, a shot cracked the still air so close to his ear as to startle and tumble him from his mount. 'Down, down, down,' he yelled instinctively as he fell. A second shot followed just as Gus crashed to the ground with a thud.

'Hit,' came a yelp followed by a second thud and a groan. It was Henry.

Another two shots cracked and thumped into the ground

behind them. Four shots in all from a rapid-fire volley.

Gus caught sight of Chrissy as she scrambled towards Henry. 'Down,' he called again as a startled horse turned, pounding hoofs as it tried to escape, but Chrissy held tight to the reins and pulled the horse after her.

'Git, go on and git, you'll not put me off my land,' came the shout from down the slope. It was Beverly Warren.

'Bev, Bev Warren, it's Gus, Sheriff Gus Ward of Laramie.'

'Gus? What are you doing here?'

'Coming to help you.'

Gus could hear the swishing sound of running legs against the saltbush as Bev and Luke arrived.

'Are you all OK?'

'Henry? Henry, you OK?' called Gus.

'Henry's hurt,' said Chrissy.

On hearing the voice, Bev said, 'Is that you, Chrissy Mayfield?'

'Yes, Mrs Warren.'

Bev hurried to her and Henry. 'Give me a look.'

Gus followed to find Henry on his back clutching his upper right arm. 'Can you move your fingers? Show me,' he asked.

Henry opened and closed his hand.

'Good. What about your elbow?'

Henry moved his forearm back and forth a little.

'Good.'

'Luke, Luke, lamp,' called Bev loudly.

Gus glanced over to catch the shape of Luke Warren shuffling back down the slope, his rifle still in his hand. He turned his attention back to Henry. 'Lift your hand from the wound and give me a look.' The light from the moon showed a dark patch of blood upon the sleeve. It wasn't as much as he feared. He put his hands around the arm and pushed his fingers into the soft flesh near the armpit to feel the bone. As he squeezed he waited for Henry to jump, but he didn't. 'You're blessed,' he said, 'the shot has missed the bone.' He moved Henry's hand back to the wound. 'Keep pressing till we can plug the hole. Can you stand? We'll get you down to the homestead.' Gus helped his son to his feet.

'Oh, my Lord, it must have been the hand of God that saved you,' said Beverly. 'Because I'm normally a good shot and so is Luke.' She put her arm around Chrissy's shoulder and squeezed. 'So good to see you, Chrissy. Bring the horses down, sweetheart, hitch them round back, there's water there.'

Under the light of an oil lamp, Henry was indeed 'lucky'. The damage from the shot was minor, causing a neat wound in the fleshy part of the upper arm, a little to the rear. The exit hole was not that far from and about the same dimension as the entry. The size of a fingertip. When washed clean, it was difficult to see how the shot had not actually entered Henry's side. He must have had his arm raised as it crossed the path of the bullet.

Bev talked Chrissy through each aspect of the attention being given, from drying and packing each puncture to the arm with a rolled cotton gauze, to the tight wrapping of the bandage. 'It's going to be sore and best it be tucked inside your shirt for the trip home.' Bev looked at Chrissy. 'You will have to help nurse him along.'

Chrissy had her arm around Henry's shoulder as she nodded her head.

'So, am I presuming correctly that we might be expecting some other folks tonight?' Bev asked Gus, as she lifted the wash bowl from the table. 'Bring the cloth, Chrissy.' They both walked across to a bench that ran along the wall next to the cast-iron stove.

'Yes, not sure when, but I don't expect long,' replied Gus.

'How many? Three? Or more?'

'Three.'

'Well, we'll be ready. Have been for a while. We've been sleeping out under the trees on watch. When we saw three horses on the crest, we just did what we planned to do. Shoot. Maybe in hindsight it was not such a good plan after all. Don't know what I'd done if I had killed any one of you. But I know one thing, I'm going to get my shotgun if I can't hit the side of a barn with my rifle.'

'Where do you and Luke sleep, Bev?' asked Gus as he looked around the homestead.

'Luke, there by the door, me back behind the divide, why?'

'We need to pad up both beds to make it look like they're occupied. I want them to enter your cabin.'

'Are we going to shoot them in here when they enter?' asked Bev.

'No, I think your plan of taking watch from under the trees is a good one. But once they enter your home unannounced and uninvited, their intentions of harm are clear.'

'Well, if that's how the law works,' concluded Bev.

Gus just said, 'In a way,' before turning to Henry. 'You just rest. Chrissy, please help Luke make up the beds. Bev, show me where you've been taking watch.'

The moon was now higher and strong enough to cast a shadow. From the hiding spot on the edge of the trees, the crest of the ridge was clearly defined and Gus wondered how the three of them had not been shot dead from this position. The distance was not much more than a hundred yards and the elevation not much more than twenty feet over that distance. To the front of the homestead, before the narrow veranda, lay a bare flat patch of ground about twenty yards wide. The moonlight seemed brightest upon this area.

It would be the killing ground.

'This will work fine,' said Gus. 'Let's assemble the troops.'

Gus checked the beds, and with the lamp extinguished, the dark shapes each represented a sleeping body. He left the front door unlocked and positioned Henry, Luke and Chrissy out in the open before the homestead, ten yards apart, so that he could pace out the range back to the trees and view them as targets. Each was clearly defined in the moonlight, including their facial features. He then asked the three of them to walk to the top of the crest of the ridge and back down to the homestead.

However, Henry said he was feeling a little light-headed and needed to sit down. Bev offered to take his place and Gus watched them walk to the crest, Chrissy leading, only to see their figures quickly duck down and come scampering back. 'They're coming,' said Bev quietly but out of breath. 'Chrissy saw them.'

'Everyone down,' directed Gus as he sank onto one knee in the shadow of the trees.

When the uncertainty of peril approaches, fear intrudes upon the bravest of hearts. This is when courage must come to the forefront not only to act, but act decisively. Yet, the wait can seem to take an eternity and this time it was almost too much to bear. Where were they? Had Chrissy got it wrong?

Gus called softly, 'Chrissy, come here.' She responded quickly and carefully so as not to make a sound as she came close. 'Are you sure you saw them?'

She leant in near to his ear, 'Sure,' she said quietly as Gus caught sight, just for a second, of three shapes, crouching low, moving across the skyline.

'They're here,' he whispered. 'All still.'

The three figures advanced to the edge of the clearing, paused for a second before each charged across the open space, guns drawn, and on to the porch. With a sharp kick of the door they were inside and the sound of furniture being booted aside could be heard. Two shots followed. Voices called, muffled and not clear enough to understand as more furniture was kicked and knocked over.

Someone moved a little behind Gus. 'Steady,' he said softly.

The door of the homestead swung open with force and the three emerged, the last one holding two unlit oil lamps. They gathered together, one crouching to ignite the lanterns as sharp, vicious words were exchanged amongst clearly heard expletives.

Gus felt a hand on his back as Bev said softly, 'Don't let them burn my home down, Gus.'

Gus slowly stood, Winchester in his hand, and the others behind him all rose to their feet. And just as he was bringing his rifle to his shoulder, he felt Henry grip and pull at his right arm.

'Feeling faint,' said Henry softly as he clutched tighter while starting to sink to the ground and pulling Gus off balance.

Chrissy stepped past Henry as he buckled and as she did, pulled the Colt .44 from his holster. Not stopping, she walked forward at a fast pace onto the open ground towards the figures in front of the Warren homestead.

'Oh Lord,' said Bev, who followed as if to bring her back.

Chrissy continued walking briskly until she was upon Cole and his half-brothers as Gus heard her say loudly, 'Who is Aaron Moy?'

All three turned their heads to look at the young girl and seemed momentarily stunned. The figure crouching by the lit lantern stood and shaded his eyes from the light as he said belligerently, 'Me, why?'

'I saw what you did to my sister,' said Chrissy, lifting her arm, her hand tightly gripping Henry's Colt.

The shot from the pistol was taken at a range of no more than five feet. The aiming point was the face, and the .44 projectile impacted just below the left nostril with ferocous force, smashing and separating the upper jaw, to drive shattered teeth and splintering bone back into the throat and upper palate.

Aaron Moy's head was flung back violently, but his eyes remained open as he started to fall. The last sight he was to see of this world was Chrissy Mayfield and the revolver she held straight and true in her hand.

His body collapsed to the ground with a dull thud.

Rufus Cole reacted first and drew his pistol from his holster just as Bev came alongside Chrissy and fired the first barrel of her shotgun.

The distance was so short that the spread of the lead pellets was tight as a fist as they punched into his lower stomach, just near the hip. Cole fell back and as he did, his handgun fired, the shot striking the ground just between Bev and Chrissy to explode dirt and dust over their boots.

Calvin Moy took fright, turned on his heels and ran off at speed. Luke nearly knocked Gus to the ground as he leapt forward, Winchester in hand, to follow the escaping Moy brother.

Henry sank to his knees with a groan, while still gripping Gus's arm.

'Let go,' called Gus, pulling his arm free so he could follow Luke. As he rounded the corner of the homestead at a race, neither Luke nor Calvin Moy were in sight. It was as if they had both vanished.

Chrissy arrived by Gus's side, still grasping Henry's Colt.